Thomas W. Kelly

**Menana**

A Romance of the Red Indians

Thomas W. Kelly

**Menana**
*A Romance of the Red Indians*

ISBN/EAN: 9783337348649

Printed in Europe, USA, Canada, Australia, Japan

Cover: Foto ©Andreas Hilbeck / pixelio.de

More available books at **www.hansebooks.com**

# MENANA;

## A ROMANCE OF THE RED INDIANS,

### IN TEN CANTOS, WITH NOTES;

TO WHICH ARE ADDED

# THE DEATH ROBE,

AND

## TWO OTHER POEMS OF THE AMERICAN WOODS;

BY

# T. W. KELLY,

AUTHOR OF "MYRTLE LEAVES," "ST. AGNES' FOUNTAIN,"
"ROSEMARY LEAVES," ETC. ETC.

———

LONDON:

PRINTED FOR AND PUBLISHED BY THE AUTHOR,
33, BEAUMONT STREET, PORTLAND PLACE, W.

MDCCCLXI.

FIVE SHILLINGS.

"Savages we call them, because their manners differ from ours, which we think the perfection of civility; they think the same of theirs."—*Franklin's Remarks concerning the North American Indians.*

" Here will we spin
Legends for them that have love-martyrs been."—*Hall's Poems*, 1648.

TO

MY MUCH-RESPECTED FRIEND,

## THE REV. W. W. CAZALET, A.M.

THE FOLLOWING PAGES

ARE INSCRIBED

BY THE AUTHOR.

THE subject selected for the poem of MENANA may, at least, claim the merit of novelty. The last two poems in this volume, on similar topics, appeared many years ago in a small privately-printed collection by the present Author, and were the only ones, he believes, of their length, then published, the materials for which were drawn from the same sources, namely, the Country of the Red or North American Indians. MENANA, written also a considerable time since, contains a more ample description of the habits and customs of those interesting tribes than either of its predecessors.

# TO MY MANUSCRIPT OF MENANA.

### I.

Ah, me! what sudden fit has seiz'd thee now,
   That thou would'st fain go wander forth abroad,
Where men thy faults shall scan, nor aught allow
   To be deserving of the slightest laud?

### II.

Beneath thy parent's roof thou long hast dwelt
   In calm contentment and unbroken ease;
Then why forsake it now, when he has felt
   So long thy presence in his leisure please?

### III.

Ah! is it wise, with high ambitious aim,
   To challenge pedants dull, or critics sour,
And roam in search of—what? some partial fame,
   To last, perchance, a year, or scarce an hour?

### IV.

Dost thou in gaudy binding wish to shine,
   The livery of each literary hack?
Better far keep within a homely shrine,
   Than strut about with gold upon thy back.

T. W. K.

# ERRATA.

Page 11, last line of note, for *Rambles* read *Rambler.*

—— 17, line 5, note, read "thickest *trees*."

—— 21, line 16, for *admidst*, read *amidst*.

—— 26, note *c*, omit the circumflex.

—— 73, line 6, for *firstling's* read *firstlings'*

—— 101, line 16, read

' Until again thy presence pleasure brought."

—— 162, line 16, for *accent* read *accents*.

# MENANA.

## CANTO I.

WILDS of the West! skirting whose virgin shore,
Huge forests rise and mighty torrents roar;
Where Mississippi rolls its stream along,                .
Rocks, mountains, woods, and sedgy banks among;
Where fruitful Florida's fair plains extend,
And Nature proves an ever-bounteous friend;
Where flowers and shrubs of every pleasing hue
By towering trees are shelter'd from the view;
Where the Magnolia in pure beauty blows,
And the bright yellow water-lily[a] glows,
Fresh from the waking languors of the night,
When it has drank the sun's first draught of light.

---

[a] Nymphæa lutea.

B

While the convolvulus sheds forth its bells,
In which the humming-bird securely dwells:
Vast scenes! where all is wild, gigantic, grand,
And countless charms bedeck a savage land;
Deep solitudes! where footsteps seldom roam,
The red man's Eden, or a hermit's home.


　　Here vernal islets viewless sails unfurl'd,
Each gently gliding, like a fairy world;
Where elfin-spirits might have held their court,
And gaily wanton'd in their mystic sport;
Islets that often floated on their way
In twin-like pairs, as seeking some bright bay,
There to unlade their blooming freight of flow'rs,
And fragrance lend to unknown blissful bow'rs.
In this rich clime, by nature boldly stamp'd,
Unspoilt by art, were native tribes encamp'd;
Amidst a host of warriors, on his throne,
A rudely elevated pile of stone,
Simaghan sat, a broad elm o'er his head,
Festoon'd with cluster'd vines, its branches spread,
Gracefully forming, in luxuriant leaf,
A canopy above the nation's chief.
A solemn dignity the Sachem wore,
And marks of honor on his figure bore;
His dress, his rank and office well bespoke;
Reaching his feet, hung down his ample cloak,

Emblazon'd with each battle he had fought,[a]
And of the hide of a young bison wrought;
His coronal, a snow-like ermine wreath,
Contrasting with the scalping-lock beneath,
Bore the proud Canieu's[b] rare and raven wing:
His neck was circled with a massive ring
Of burnish'd gold, with coral studs inlaid;
His ears the rarest pendent pearls display'd;
And on his painted breast, depending low,
A chain of bear-claws hung in double row;
A beaded buck-skin belt confin'd his waist,
To which a splendid tomahawk was brac'd;
Girt were his giant limbs with leggings blue,
Seen when apart his outer robe he drew;
The jaguar's hide supplied his arrow's sheath,
And grisly hung the sever'd head beneath;
At ankle height his mocassins[c] were bound
With quills of porcupine and shells edg'd round;
While on his war-club leaning, thus attir'd,
His dark eye's glance a silent awe inspir'd;

---

[a] "This robe, with its tracings on it, is the chart of his military life."—*Catlin's Notes of the North American Indians.*

[b] The feathers of this bird, the *Falco-fulvus* of *Linnæus*, and *Ring-tail Eagle of Wilson*, are highly esteemed by the Indians. No person is permitted to wear them who has not been engaged with an enemy: a horse is sometimes given for a feather of this bird.— *Halkett's Historical Notes respecting the Indians of North America, &c.*

[c] Mocassins are a sort of Indian buskins.

Nor less expressive in his manly face
Beam'd the peculiar features of his race.

Near to the Sachem,[a] 'neath the same green tree,
Menana[b] sat, a maid of high degree,
His only daughter, or believed to be;
Hiding her graces, as sweet violets do
Their meek and modest petals, from the view;
Her beauteous hair magnolia[c] flowerets crown'd,
Which, as she mov'd, breath'd redolence around;
Bracelets of gold[d] adorned her wrists; her zone
With colour'd beads of sparkling brightness shone;
And, wrought of mulberry-bark, a white robe[e] grac'd
Her lovely shoulders, loose, below her waist;

---

[a] *Sachem;* one to whom all the others owe some kind of fealty or subjection.—*Hutchinson's History of Massachuset's Bay.*

[b] " *Menana,*" a North American Indian name, which means *the Daughter of the Flood.*—*Tales of an Indian Camp.*

[c] The smaller flowers of these chaste and odoriferous blossoms are sometimes selected and formed into wreaths for the hair, to deck the wife of some heroic chieftain.

[d] Golden ornaments were worn by persons in authority as a mark of distinction. " They had among them, besides their king, a degree of nobility who were more elegant in their dresses, particularly their hair, which they formed in various shapes, and adorned with the finest feathers they could procure; from their ears hung large pearls, round their necks they wore chains, and armlets of pearl."—*Pinkerton.* " They wore bracelets and ear-rings of fine pearls."—*Hennepin's New Discovery*, page 177.

[e] " Her white robe of mulberry-bark floated loosely behind her."
— *The Natchez*, vol. i

In feathery woof[a] and quaintly fashioned gear,
She seem'd a being of a radiant sphere;
Whose light aërial figure one might deem
Some sweet creation of a lover's dream;
Still brighter seeming from the contrast round
Of those swarth warriors, wrapt in mood profound,
Assembled on that spot, to guard or wait
Upon their Chieftain in his wonted state:
They, a wild, cunning, rude, and daring band;
She, simple, lovely, graceful, meek and bland,
Tender in heart as elegant in form,
With woman's feelings, gentle, pure and warm:
Slender she was, symmetrical in growth;
Like to the palm, or reed, or blending both;
The palm in stately dignity of frame,
The reed in all that gentleness should claim.

Behold, around, what earnest crowds repair,
With shouts tumultuous echoing through the air;
So loud the din, it seem'd as 'twould have rent
The azure curtains of the firmament;
And where the distant hills seem in the skies
To melt away, more multitudes arise;
In long canoes some steer towards the land,
And thronging numbers line the pebbled strand;

---

[a] "Our women wrought feathery blankets for the winter, and mulberry mantles for the summer."—*History of Louisiana*, page 44. See also *Pinkerton's Voyages.*

Till, marshall'd in one mighty host, they reach
From plains afar down to the billowy beach:
Some tribes the tomahawk and hatchet wield;
Others, the massive club and ponderous shield;
Some, bear-skin mantles o'er their shoulders fling;
And their long maple-bows behind them sling;
Some, wicker-armour[a] wear; some, ample vests
Of broad fur bound upon their painted breasts;
And some have sheaves of arrows, form'd for speed,
Of the elastic, light Virginian reed,
Grown on the banks of the Ohio river,
And crystal-pointed[b] in each thong-bound quiver.
Brightly their weapons glitter in the sun,
Foreboding deeds of import to be done;
Some feats of triumph meet for battle-day,
While yells and antics rude their zeal display.
Meanwhile, high whirl'd in air, their spears keep time
To the wild war-dance and discordant chime.

But who is he whose feathers backward stream,
Wave in the wind and brighten in the beam?

---

[a] " Some, for defence, bore shields made of the bark of trees, and a kind of wicker-armour, which they made use of in time of war."— *Pinkerton's Voyages.* Also *Raynal's History of the East and West Indies.*

[b] Some of the arrows used by the North American Indians are made of reeds; they are pointed with wood and headed with splinters of crystal, or something sharp.—*Pinkerton's Voyages.*

Tekarrah![a] he whose name has often spread
Throughout the camp of foes a sudden dread;
Who feigns all forms,[b] the wariest to surprise,
As brave in arms as cunning in disguise,
Who needs but few to put a host to flight,
As the sun's dawn dispels the clouds of night.
In the lone wigwam, o'er the watch-fire's flame,
The stoutest hearts would startle at his name;
And many fearful tales his foes recite,
Of deeds that baffled all their craft and might,
Struggles in which his arm terrific fell,
And only left the slain its weight to tell;
Or if a leaf but rustled from a tree,
Women would start and half exclaim, " 'Tis he!"
Or let a stranger's mocassin but sound
Its tinkling bell[c] on the adjacent ground,
Instantly rous'd, some straight would to the grass
Apply their ear, to list what steps might pass;[d]

---

[a] *Tekarrah i. e.* αγγελος, *Messenger of the Great Spirit.—Note to Tales of an Indian Camp.*

[b] Many remarkable anecdotes are recorded of their cunning and artifice to surprise and ensnare their enemies. One of their common tricks was to envelope themselves in the skins of different animals, the bison, the hog, &c.

[c] They sew hawk-bells and small pieces of tin to their mocassins. —*Long's Voyage*, page 36.

[d] The acuteness of hearing which characterizes the North American Indians is truly wonderful. Many of them can hear footsteps at the distance of four or five hours' journey, and tell, by

Then seek, with vengeance kindled in their eyes,
Fire-bark[a] to give the signal of surprise.
Some from their belts would grasp, with eager haste,
The gleaming knife, or hatchet firmly brac'd;
Or, only half withdrawn, the steel retain
Till summon'd forth to bear a crimson stain;
Others would madly whirl the ready blade,
And shout the war-whoop through the forest-glade.

Onward he comes! a long-continued shout
Dispell'd the cautious Sachem's secret doubt.
He wears a silver gorget, deck'd with beads,
The badge and proof of many valiant deeds;
And which in fight had oft repell'd the force
Of poison'd arrows in their deadly course.
A tuft of hair,[b] of scarlet colour dyed,
With pearl-shells clasp'd, above each wrist is tied,
And in his wampum-girdle,[c] which confines
His robes of fur, a polish'd hatchet shines.

---

murmurs inaudible to an European ear, at what distance the enemy is, by clapping their ears to the ground.—See *Chateaubriand's Travels in America.*

  [a] Fire-bark—*Scotus Wigwas.*—See *Long's Travels.*

  [b] "They adorn themselves with little locks of fine red hair."—*De la Sale's Second Voyage in North America.* "It is usually taken from the knee of the buffalo (bison); no person wears it that has not distinguished hi : self in the field.—*Weld's Travels.*

  [c] Wampum, small beads manufactured from shells strung upon sinews, and united for this purpose.—*Service of Indians in Civilized*

With eye commanding and with gesture proud,
He steps undaunted 'midst the exulting crowd;
Untaught to purchase safety with disgrace,
His mien is worthy of the Natchez race;
His jetty locks hang o'er his manly cheek,
And through his eyes his soul appears to speak;
Athletic are his limbs; his fearless brow
Attests a spirit nought can break or bow.
He comes! the captive born to add one more
To triumphs Simaghan had gain'd before;
And Simaghan was eager to behold
An enemy so wary and so bold;
To feast his sight upon the daring youth,
And steel his heart to gentleness and ruth;
For now the Council, after long debate,
Had fix'd by solemn doom Tekarrah's fate;
Though yet two intervening days must pass,
While in slow progress moves the dingy mass,
Ere it can reach the place of sacrifice,
And bid the death-flame on the altar rise.

The Sachem rose, with him Menana too,
And both with stately dignity withdrew;

---

*Warfare*, 1827. On formal occasions, or in acts of ceremony, the Indians accompany every important speech with an appropriate belt, consisting of different coloured beads, strung together. These belts constitute, in fact, the records of each tribe, and the speeches delivered by the chiefs in connexion with the wampum. Belts are handed down by tradition.

But first, with graceful air he wav'd his hand,
Well understood, a signal of command;
And bade the multitude that throng'd in sight,
Encamp within the forest for the night;
Recruit their strength, their vengeful ire renew,
And with the morning's light their course pursue;
To them his patriarchal word was law,
And all the tribes obey'd with reverent awe.

Now keenly turn'd he, as to recognize
The youthful warrior in his noble prize.
Few were his guards; for many, worn and weak,
Were fain some brief and needful rest to seek.
And now it was, till then with pain conceal'd,
Menana's wretchedness was first reveal'd,
First struck the aged Sachem's piercing eye,
Who little dream'd the cause, and wondered why
Her eyes, her cheeks, her inmost grief betray'd,
As he her downcast looks awhile survey'd.
So pale and quivering, she was chang'd as much
As flowerets blighted by the hot wind's touch.
He gaz'd, but spake not, yet to speak inclin'd,
While varying thoughts were passing in his mind.
It could not sudden illness be; ah, no!
Her weeping bade him that surmise forego.
Doubtful, perplex'd, her youthful handmaids nigh,
He beckon'd forth, and left her with a sigh;
Back to her wattled-hut her virgin train

In mute attendance led the maid again.
But soon their painful presence she forbade,
And wander'd forth alone, and careless stray'd,
She knew not whither; all her aim to flee
From her own thoughts, replete with misery,
Where her young spirit first to love had wak'd,
That gentle spirit now with anguish ach'd.
How alter'd seem'd the aspect of each scene
Where'er Tekarrah by her side had been!
For memory over each its shadow threw,
And chang'd to darkness every brilliant hue.
Either by secret sympathy, or chance,
The maid, absorb'd in deep bewildering trance,
Her steps directed to the guarded ground,
Where lay her prostrate lover strongly bound.
" Menana! 'tis herself!" the chieftain cried,
" Oh, turn not from me, nor thy pity hide;
" Think not at ills like this I feel dismay,
" Or envy now my foes their prosperous day;
" But when I undertook this last emprize,
" The sun forewarn'd me and forsook the skies[a];
" The white bird flew before me on my road,[b]
" With fluttering wing my danger to forebode.

---

[a] The Indians never perform any business except the sky be
clear.—*Latrobe's Rambles in North America.*

[b] If the white bird flies with frightened wing before the traveller,
it forebodes danger to him.—See *Chateaubriand's Travels.*

" Look up, Menana! do not weep for me;
" E'en yet kind Destiny may set me free.
" Against the rapids I will steer my course,
" Or a sure path through trackless forests force.
" Too well thou know'st I was before betray'd
" Into a deep-laid, wily ambuscade.
" Regardless of the Manitou of dreams[a],
" Who governs all as fit to him beseems.
" Yet, though my foes were fierce, and fell their hate,
" They deem'd it prudent not revenge to sate,
" But held my life in pledge, until restor'd,
" By us the chief detain'd, by them deplor'd;
" 'Twas then I saw thee first, and first ador'd;
" Nor can I e'er forget what new delight
" Enwrapt my soul, entranc'd my ardent sight!
" As, from the root the stem becomes a tree,
" So has my love increas'd in growth for thee;
" As rivers swell to torrents in their course,
" So has my love augmented all its force;
" As on a moss-bed sparks ignite to flame,
" So quick my passion kindled at thy name;
" And when my fitful fancy, duly taught,
" Has conjur'd up thy vision'd form to thought,
" What charms and sweetness have in thee appear'd,
" And, oh! thy presence made each scene endear'd!

---

[a] Among the numerous tribes of North American Indians, the Supreme Being is designated by many names; but all having the same signification.

" I deem'd, at leaf-fall, we would stray alone,

" To hear the winds make melancholy moan ;

" Or chase the swallow skimming o'er the plain,

" As if it dar'd us to pursuit—in vain;

" Or watch the arch that crowns the misty hill,

" Its blending hues in one bright bow distil.

" I thought thee beautiful as was the fawn,

" When graceful bounding o'er the sloping lawn ;

" And, in my dreams, I saw a milk-white dove[a],

" The surest omen of a happy love.

" In vain I strove my bosom's flame to quench,

" In vain thine image from my soul to wrench.

" Hopeless the task ! I liv'd for thee alone,

" And dar'd at last my fervid transport own.

" Fierce as the sun, as southern tempests strong,

" It hurl'd me with impetuous force along.

" Yet ere at length I ventur'd to disclose

" To thee the hapless story of my woes,

" What pangs I underwent that others' eyes

" Might pierce not love's, alas ! constrain'd disguise !

" The eagle, struck, beneath his wing may hide

" The arrow's point within his bleeding side ;

---

[a] It was a tradition among some of the North American Indians that the souls of the good, after their entrance upon the land of never-ceasing happiness, were transformed into doves. The dove is also among them, as elsewhere, an emblem of meekness. " And his soul is the soul of the dove."—Vide " *The Idols*," *a Tradition of the Ricaras.*.

" So I concealed the pain I bore for thee,
" Beneath a brow that veil'd my misery.
" Nay; bid me not of danger now beware—
" A captive cougar in the hunter's snare,
" Or elk that from the salt-spring turns away,
" Mark'd by the gaunt grey-wolf, his destin'd prey,
" Is such as I.——But, oh! for gentle love,
" What perils would not sun-born spirits prove!
" Yet dangers past should be with joys repaid:
" Then marvel not I seek thy love, dear maid!
" The sweetest balm to soothe all human smart
" Is the fond sympathy of woman's heart;
" And can I meet thy blue eyes' pensive ray
" With thought of danger lurking in the way?
" No! love would kindle courage from despair,
" O'erleap all barriers, and all hazards dare.
" Blossom of life! let good or ill betide,
" Ne'er would I quit thee for the world beside;
" But, like a dove that guards its tender mate,
" Would o'er thee watch in every change of fate!"

At this, Menana's eyes, with love o'erfraught,
Turn'd on the chief, long cherish'd in her thought;
While hope shed on her heart a fitful gleam,
As light through clouds will, penetrating, stream.
Her look betray'd a melting tenderness!
But was it love? Oh, could it be aught less?
Or was it pity waken'd in her breast?
And pity is to love akin confest.

Yes; in her gentle heart, with pity fraught,
Love now was, like some fairy fabric, wrought.
Whate'er her feelings only time could show,
But plainly now that look betoken'd woe.
Some words she falter'd, but so indistinct,
They seem'd as by no conscious meaning link'd.
The only sign her swollen heart could make,
Was one to tell him that it soon would break.
Then she to Heaven uprais'd her streaming eyes,
And clasp'd her hands in fearful agonies;
'Till, with a sudden bound, she darted hence,
Leaving the captive tortured with suspense.

Too inexperienc'd, hapless one! to know
What bitters Fate may in Life's goblet throw.
How little didst thou dream, fond-hearted maid!
What grief would soon thy inmost soul invade;
Whilst lately sitting where the lilies slake
Their opening petals in the purple lake,
Whose waves to kiss thy feet seem'd gently led,
But, loth to stain their whiteness, backward fled!
Who that had seen thee bathing at the side
Of that clear water where the rocks divide
And form a screen, could then have prophesied
Thy cheek so soon would lose its roseate dye,
And dim become the lustre of thine eye?
That, ere the eve its amber shades should throw
Where golden coronals of blossoms grow—

That, ere those lovely flowers had kiss'd the stream,
And clos'd their yellow cups till morning's beam,
Thy heart, Menana, should be fast ensnar'd,
By love enchain'd, for misery unprepar'd?
Oh! had'st thou been the gentle victim spar'd!

Ye virgin handmaids, who around her smile,
And fain would all her secret pain beguile;
Behold her hair dishevell'd o'er her brows:
Look, how she twines those slips of cypress boughs:
See, how she strips the branches leaf by leaf.
Oh! strive to rouse her from this trance of grief,
And minister, with all your tender art,
Some blest elixir to her aching heart.

Ye matrons, too, who mingled with the band
Of warlike chiefs and elders of the land,
Witness'd how pale she turn'd, how wildly glanc'd,
As in the train the captive youth advanc'd;
You saw her humid eyes of azure hue,
Like lotus-flowerets newly bath'd in dew;
Nor fail'd to mark that half-unconscious gaze
That fixed on him its concentrated rays;
That gaze so tearful, yet so bright withal—
A sun-burst sparkling through a waterfall.

E'en now her footsteps to the groves repair,
While soothing stillness only hovers there.

Goes she to muse in twilight solitude—
To weep in silence, and in secret brood?
Her heart, alas! (though not her lips confess)
Heaves the deep sigh and sadly answers, yes!

Beneath the Sumach's canopy of leaves,
The wild swan to the sweet embankment cleaves;
From bow'r and bush blue nightingales enchain[a]
The souls of flowers, that listen to their strain,
And blushing roses fragrantly incline
Their heads to listen to the song divine.
Warm in his happy nest the amorous dove
Woos his coy-mate to share the bliss of love
While round about them, like a playful child,
Each leafy bough sports wantonly and wild;
And Nature seems not to rejoice the less
For poor Menana's hopeless wretchedness.
In vain amidst the woods she vents her grief;
Nor shade nor solitude affords relief,
Nor slumber steals the harass'd sense to sleep,
And feverish madness from her brain to keep.

---

[a] "That sort of nightingale that I saw is of a peculiar form; for it is a lesser size than the European, and of a bluish colour, and its notes are more diversified; besides that, it lodges in the holes of trees, and four or five of them commonly keep together upon the thickest, and with joint notes warble over their songs."— See *Pinkerton's Voyages*. Mrs. Jameson probably alludes to this bird when she writes, " The lovely blue-bird, with its brilliant violet plumage."—See her *Winter Studies and Summer Rambles in Canada*.

Martyr to Love and Fate beyond control,
Tekarrah's doom alone absorbs her soul.
'Tis this which makes her in such anguish bow;
'Tis this which stamps such horror on her brow.
Should she to Simaghan her cause refer,
Would he on such a theme list e'en to *her?*
The sudden thought reviv'd her from despair;
She could but fail—she only had to dare.

While thus she ponder'd, heedless where she stray'd,
Low plaintive murmurs issued near the shade.
O'er a new mound, a trodden path beside[a]
(That once had serv'd two nations to divide),
Where grew sweet nursling plants, but newly set[b],
Memorials of affection and regret,
And where the festoon'd pine-plant intertwin'd,
Shedding its blossoms to the passing wind,
A mother kneels and weeps, with bitter cries,
Her darling offspring borne to starry skies;
Upward, with anxious hope, her eye directs,
And fondly yet his blest return expects,

---

[a] We were passing the tomb of an infant, which served as a boundary between two nations, and was placed, according to custom, by the road-side, that the young women who were going to the neighbouring fountain might, as they passed, endeavour to allure to their bosoms the spirit of the innocent creature, and restore it to its country."—*Chateaubriand.*

[b] The same custom formerly prevailed in our country. It is noticed by Shakspere, as part of the funeral ceremonies, that flowers, herbs, &c. were strewed over the grave.

Deeming his slumbering spirit in some hour
Of moonlight stillness, when no night-clouds lour,
Might back to earth be wafted on the breeze
Of fragrant incense from the wild spice trees.
Now strewing flowers, her memory weaves the spell
Of one sad thought on which it loves to dwell;
Her infant's image floats before her mind,
She hears his voice in every whispering wind.
Poor simple thing! by phantasies possess'd,
No more she'll clasp him to her throbbing breast.

Menana felt for that poor mother's grief,
And fain had proffer'd, though in vain, relief;
Yet, while her heart was still to pity prone,
It harbour'd woes more poignant of her own.
In vain her feelings to suppress she strove—
But what shall quell the strength of woman's love?
On bended knees, she breath'd to Heaven a pray'r,
Then sunk again, relapsing in despair.
Too well she knew his foes had seal'd the doom
Of him alone she lov'd, in fatal gloom;
Too well she knew Tekarrah was to die
Ere two more suns should gild the western sky.
Yet she resolv'd her sire to supplicate,
E'en though his love for her should turn to hate.
With purpose fix'd, and hurrying steps, she went
Straightway to seek the Sachem in his tent.

**END OF CANTO THE FIRST.**

# MENANA.

---

## CANTO II.

---

" The very first
Of human life must spring from woman's breast,
Your first small words are taught you from her lips,
Your first tears quench'd by her, and your last sighs
Too often breath'd out in a woman's hearing,
When men have shrunk from the ignoble care
Of watching the last hour of him who led them."

BYRON.

---

FAST to a pine-tree was Tekarrah bound,
His weary guards compos'd themselves around;
For rest they needed on their toilsome way,
Their ancient laws and customs to obey.
Daily they halted with the setting sun,
And now they soundly slept, save only one,
Who watch'd the captive did not burst the knot
Of osier-bands that fix'd him to the spot.
The mighty throng dispers'd as each was bent,
The old to rest, the young for merriment.
Here, lively mirth proclaim'd youth's buoyant reign;
There, white-rob'd maidens tripp'd along the plain;

And many a swarthy form in torpor lay,
Subdu'd by fire-drink's[a] dire, destructive sway.
At intervals the funeral-song was heard,
In distance broken by the plaintive gourd[b].

What sounds are those that through the foliage steal?
What form is that the opening boughs reveal?
'Tis woman's voice that breaks upon the ear,
'Tis woman's self that stands the captive near.
A matron thus the startled chief address'd,
And by her words disturbed his tranquil breast:

" Shame to the remnant of thy nation's band,
" Thus to have left thee to the victor's brand!
" Would thou had'st fallen by a warrior's blow,
" And thus in death been honor'd by a foe!
" But destin'd soon to be engulph'd in fire,
" Admidst exulting shouts thou wilt expire.
" Caution or craft thou should'st have had, at least,
" The common instinct of the simple beast;
" True, the wild bounding Bison knows no fear,
" But reckless plunges on the hunter's spear,
" When the fierce animal might safely hide,
" And shun the steel that rips his bleeding side.

---

[a] Brandy.

[b] The Chechikoué. Gourds were converted into musical instruments, capable of emitting a variety of tones.—See *Joutel's Journal of De la Sale's last Voyage to the Gulph of Mexico.*

" He who is rashly bold, is rarely free
" From fatal risk against an enemy.
" The Cougar crouches, hush'd his every gasp,
" Until he finds his prey within his grasp.
" Enough to undertake, had'st thou been wise,
" The perils of the hunter's enterprise;
" For he, if foil'd, or should he hunger know,
" Against some tent has but to hang his bow,
" Claim hospitality, and be receiv'd
" With welcome, and his wants all straight reliev'd.
" Avails it now thou wert in battle brave?
" Those feet, that may have press'd thy father's grave,
" Those hands, that rais'd the helpless in their need,
" Or dress'd the wounded, or the captive freed,
" Those eyes that now reflect the glowing mind,
" Are doom'd to feel each cruelty refined;
" Thine ashes, too, shall on the winds be blown,
" Thy deeds forgotten, and thy name unknown.
" Or should a tomb be to thy bones allow'd,
" No mourning kindred will around it crowd;
" But thither shall insulting foes resort,
" And children o'er it trample in their sport.
" Far better had'st thou, like some floweret, shed
" Life's fragrance, ere thine infant days had fled—
" Resign'd thy spirit pure as first 'twas sent
" To animate thy earthy tenement.
" Yes, hadst thou breath'd thy last in childhood's years,
" Thy grave had drank a mother's sacred tears.

" There, strew'd by her with lilies and with maize,[a]
" The young had paus'd to sigh, the old to gaze;
" There, too, some winding, tangled path beside,
" Had virgins stopp'd their bashfulness to hide,
" While fondly wooing love's supreme caress,
" Their arms in time maternally to bless—
" Bless with a lovely girl, a cherub-boy,
" Pledges of union, harmony and joy.
" But not like buds, to perish ere they bloom,
" Or meet, like thee, an ignominious doom.
" No flower had there in modest sweetness blush'd,
" While all around in calm repose was hush'd,
" But young and lovely lips its breath had woo'd,
" To charm away the spell of maidenhood.[b]
" There still would linger long the rosy bride,
" And kiss each bud she deem'd to thee allied,
" Seeking thy essence, fragrant, fresh and warm,
" As first instill'd into thy tender form;
" Or else transform'd into a pure-white dove,[c]
" To bless a second time maternal love.

---

[a] " *Joutel's Journal of De La Sale's Last Voyage*, 1714," and other works on North America.

[b] The Red Indian women have a belief that the spirits of children who die are embalmed in the breath of flowers.—*Chateaubriand's Travels*, vol. i, p. 213.

[c] Vide note of page 13

For these superstitions alluded to, see the various writers on the North American Indians.

" Yes, had'st thou closed thy days in cradled sleep,
" No eyes would now thy adverse fortunes weep ;
" Nor hadst thou then disgrac'd thy father's name,
" Or on thy race have cast a coward's shame ! "


She ceas'd. " Thine are the words of truth," he said :
" Man from his birth receives kind woman's aid ;
" Receives it still from infancy to death,
" And with her sighs is mix'd his parting breath.
" Grateful as plants for dews at morn or eve,
" Thy consolations, matron, I receive.
" But now, of what avail were it to tell
" By what mischance within these toils I fell ;
" Some men, like dwarfish shrubs, are mean and low,
" While others like the stately cedars grow.
" The boy, as nature prompts, pursues his plan ;
" The paddle or the bow bespeaks the man.
" You deem him happy who forbears to roam
" Beyond his wattled hut or forest home,
" Who seeks no conflict and who finds no foes ;
" Yet even *he* has many untold woes.
" Still, should he be in that condition blest,
" Let war but kindle ardour in his breast,
" His soul expands, his manly spirit burns,
" He pants in rage, and sloth-like quiet spurns.
" A plant there is that in our forest grows,
" Whose flower doth ne'er its virgin buds disclose :

" Its name is *Hope;*[a] so in the timid frame
" Sleeps on the plant of life—still, still the same.
" But like a stout canoe whirl'd down the tide,
" The warrior rushes with heroic pride;
" Wherever danger points, or fame can charm,
" Or home or kindred urge his potent arm."


Thus far the chief had spoken, when a sound
The matron heard, and vanish'd at a bound;
And now before him stood a lovely maid,
In trinkets bright and feathers rare array'd,
One he had noted in Menana's train ;
But comes she also to deride his pain?
She paus'd a moment, as oppress'd and weak,
And thus essay'd with trembling voice to speak:


" So young, so graceful, and so soon to die !
" Would I could save him from such destiny !
" Methinks I'd hide him in some flowery haunt,
" As in the scroll-leaf[b] of the water-plant
" The little gold-eyed frog lies safe conceal'd,
" To no fierce, dangerous enemy reveal'd.

---

[a] " Man cherishes in his bosom a desire of happiness, which is neither destroyed nor fulfilled: there is in our forests a plant, the flower of which never opens—it is Hope."—*The Natchez.* vol i, p. 31. The plant here alluded to is said to be *Hopea Tinctoria.*

[b] " This plant is, I believe," says Chateaubriand, " the same as the lotus, a kind of Nenuphar."—See also *Latrobe's Rambler in North America*, vol. ii, page 49.

" Forsaken captive! where thy place of birth?
" Thy mother who? and what thy deeds of worth?
" Who was thy sire, and from what nation sprung?
" Was thine the mossy cradle lightly hung,
" Suspended to the boughs of maple-trees,
" And gently rock'd by every murmuring breeze?
" Say, wert thou nestled in those balmy bowers,
" Which, softly waving, seem like snowy flowers?[a]
" Did loving kindred meet and give thy name
" O'er fires that burnt with aromatic flame?[b]
" Perchance, thou oft hast witness'd in thy sleep
" A milk-white hind?[c] Thou hast: thy blushes deep[d]
" And earth-bent eye persuade me that the grove
" And lonely vale have whisper'd thee to love.
" Say, hast thou left a bride, as fair as true,
" Thy doubtful fate with boding heart to rue;
" Whose weeping eyes and loose dishevell'd hair
" Proclaim thy absence and her mute despair?

---

[a] The red maple (*acer rubrum*) grows in abundance in several places. Its leaves are white or silvery on the under sides, and when agitated by the wind, they make the tree appear as if it were full of white flowers.—*Pinkerton's Voyages*, vol. xiii, page 582.

[b] On particular occasions the Indians make a burning pile of fragrant woods.—See *Chateaubriand's Travels*, vol. i, page 211.

[c] C'était ensuite mille autres questions sur l'état de mon cœur: elles me demandoient si j'avois vu une biche blanche dans mes songes, et si les arbres de la vallée secrète m'avoient conseillé d'aimer.—*Atala.*

[d] La rougeur est sensible chez les jeunes sauvages.—Note to *Atala.*

" What if to her the wakon-bird[a] disclose
" Thy present thraldom and impending woes?
" E'en now she wistful lists thy step again!
" Futile her wishes and her hopes how vain!
" No more thou wilt to her lone arms return,
" Thy doom it is to die and her's to mourn;
" But in the happy hunting-grounds[b] above,
" Ye yet may meet again in endless love."


The chief survey'd the maid with steadfast eye,
And thus with stifled feeling made reply:
" The sweet sap flowing from the maple-tree
" Is not so welcome as thy words to me;
" Pleas'd as the swallow flies to greenwood bowers
" To dwell with sunny beams and smiling flowers,
" Joyous as rice-birds to the west repair
" To bright Savannas and a warmer air,
" Am I, amidst my fiercest foes, to find
" In thee a heart so gentle and so kind;

---

[a] The wakon-bird, in their language, is the Bird of the Great Spirit.—*Morse.* It is held by the Indians in the utmost veneration. —*Tales of an Indian Camp,* vol. iii, page 15. In critical circumstances, the sorcerers affirm that Kitchi-manitou appears above the clouds, borne by his favourite bird the wakon, a species of Bird of Paradise, with brown wings, and a tail adorned with four long green and red feathers.—*Chateaubriand's Travels,* vol. i, page 246.

[b] The land of souls.

" Oh ! wert thou sent, the virgin of last love,[a]

" Not to deride my sorrows, but remove ?

" To cheer the prospect of my speedy doom,

" And arm my soul to meet a fiery tomb ?

" To teach me death is but the path to bliss,

" A starry world far happier than this ?

" Whate'er the motive that hath brought thee here,

" Thine eyes are mild and sparkling with a tear.

" Thou art not come to mock a captive slave,

" Or wreak a woman's vengeance on the brave.

" Say, wert thou sent by one whose looks of late

" Gave token of an interest in my fate ?

" Ah ! would Menana listen to my tale,

" My lips should breathe it like the softest gale.

" Would that her heart's young slender roots incline

" In fond embrace to cling round those of mine !

" To her own beauty she herself is blind,

" As the rich silk-worm in its cell confin'd.

" Her bosom, chaste as is the snowy flake,

" Heaves like the gentle billows of the lake ;

" Her neck and shoulders as the swan's-down white ;

" Her eyes, the dove's, as soft, but, oh ! more bright !

" Her foot and hand such small proportions bear,

" The ring-dove's wing might with their size compare ;

" And when she speaks, her very tones are such,

" I could not hear nor she express too much !

---

[a] That virgin who is sent to the prisoner of war to enchant the horrors of his impending fate.

" Tell her I come, descended from a race
" That never felt dismay, nor knew disgrace.
" E'en now I feel the spirit of my sire,
" And laugh to scorn the conqueror in his ire.
" My flesh may quiver at the burning stake,
" But firmness never shall my breast forsake ;
" Though fierce devouring flames my limbs consume,
" Tekarrah's soul shall triumph o'er his doom.
" Say to the daughter of bold Simaghan,
" Though soon to perish 'neath her father's ban,
" I hate not *all* his race—oh, no ! there's one
" For whom I yet could wish these bonds undone !
" Whose smile would nerve me, were I once more free,
" With giant strength and matchless energy.
" Menana's name should through the woods resound,
" Awaking echo from her depths profound ;
" That name to me of talismanic pow'r,
" My guardian-spell in danger's fitful hour ;
" That name on which my tongue should ever dwell,
" My blood inflame and all my courage swell ! "
He ceas'd his words, and found himself alone ;
His lovely, soothing visitant had flown.

With mind bewilder'd and fatigu'd in frame,
He now requir'd repose, and slumber came.
Yet then a smile was playing on his lips,
That augur'd not his setting sun's eclipse ;
Some fond remembrance flash'd across his brain,

To give returning sense a keener pain—
Some rainbow vision cloth'd in magic hues :
Alas ! how different from his waking views !
Perchance he pictur'd, in his dreamy thought,
A scene of nuptial joy by fancy wrought;
A happy wigwam, a devoted wife,
And the sweet offspring of a wedded life;
The eager chase, or smooth inviting wave,
Deeming himself no more a captive slave.
Sleep on ! brave Natchez ! undisturb'd, alone,
Few hours thou hast on earth to call thine own.

Just as the earliest dawn of morning broke,
Tekarrah from his pleasing slumbers woke ;
Sounds, first at distance heard, became more clear,
Voices and music caught his listening ear,
Which to the ground he bent, as if to guess
Their meaning in that unknown wilderness ;
Then (while his guards were mute) upon his view
A group of lovely maidens near him drew;
And as they in each virgin grace advanc'd,
They with wild song and native gestures danc'd;
Slow was their motion, measur'd was their pace,
But mute compassion mark'd each sun-stain'd face;
Yet in their living, sparkling, jet-black eyes,
There were not wanting latent sympathies ;
For youthful valour, by misfortune press'd,
Vibrates the tenderest chord in woman's breast.

But why this seeming mockery, and why
Are proffer'd gifts to one so soon to die?
For food, the various produce of the chase
Is tender'd with a ceremonious grace.
Superior to the rest, one maiden shone,
Who seem'd to claim their reverence alone;
But o'er her face a veil was loosely plac'd,
Through which her features might not well be trac'd;
Oh! 'tis Menana! with a bursting heart,
And tears that from her eyes unbidden start,
She for the captive's life her own would pay,
Yet cautious lest she should her thoughts betray;
'Tis she who bids the rude repast be brought,
For well she knew his strength had been o'erwrought;
'Tis she whose looks induce him now to eat
The pounded maize-cake and the bison-meat;[a]
'Tis she by whom sagamité[b] is pour'd,
And proffer'd in the simple hollow'd gourd;
And, oh! 'tis she to whom his eyes address
The feelings that his tongue may not express.
Yes, 'twas Menana who before him stood,
The loveliest of that lovely sisterhood;

---

[a] The delicious dish compounded of corn and bison-meat.—
*Tales of an Indian Camp*, vol. ii, page 117.

[b] *Sagamité;* made with maize flour, sweetened with syrup of the
maple-tree. "To my taste," says Du Pratz, "it surpassed the best
dish in France."

Her graceful form, enshrin'd in spotless vest,
Beam'd with a beauty far beyond the rest,
And he, Tekarrah, well had mark'd her mien,
Through which an anxious boding might be seen
By eyes of love, and such Tekarrah's were,
E'en in that moment of his heart's despair;
Yet still she strove her bosom's pangs to veil,
And breath'd her sighs in secret to the gale;
Save that some handmaids, more observant, saw
Her troubled mood, whom straight she bade withdraw,
That she might 'scape their penetrating gaze;
Then left the captive in profound amaze.

Pensive she stray'd where roses wildly grew,[a]
And from their stems she, lingering, pluck'd a few;
These she entwin'd and circled in a wreath,
As if to be the coronal of death:[b]
Or, has she weav'd them for her own pale brow?
Ah, no! 'twas too disturb'd to wear them now;
Her mind had grown bewilder'd by her grief,
But such employment gave, perhaps, relief;
One moment, horror seiz'd upon her brain;
The next, some hope sprung up as brief as vain.
If reason re-assum'd a transient sway,
It shed upon her soul no certain ray;

---

[a] There are only four kinds of roses indigenous to North America.
—*Donn's Hortus Cantabrigiensis.*

[b] A wreath of jasmine flowers.

Yet still she nurs'd that fatal love within,
Which conscience pure would oft condemn as sin;
Thus lone and listlessly she wander'd on,
Unheeding whither, like a mateless swan,
To where the mighty Mississippi flow'd,
In all its grandeur, with its verd'rous load:
Huge trees, inur'd the raging storm to brave,
Were headlong borne upon the bounding wave;
Islets she saw, like stately cygnets, glide,
Obstructing, yet adorning too, the tide;
She gaz'd upon them, but with vacant eye,
While others yet more lovely floated by;
Each like a sylvan bow'r or blest retreat,
Or Paradise untrod by human feet;
On these the maple scarlet blossoms threw,
And yellow lilies like pavilions grew.
A thousand plants besides, commingling bright,
Perfum'd the breezes and bewitch'd the sight;
'Midst lotus-leaves green spangled serpents lay,
Basking and coiling in the sunny ray;
Luxuriant vines, entwining tree with tree,
Hung their ripe fruit in clusters heavily;
While countless birds, of brilliant plumage, sent
Their joyous music to the firmament;
Giving enchantment to those moving bowers;
Sweet, happy voyagers in barks of flowers!
Rich isles! that woo'd the zephyr's fond caress,
And seem'd to revel in voluptuousness;

So smoothly gliding, wafted by the gale,
Like Pleasure's palaces, in gentle sail.

   A scene like this, so beautifully wild,
O'er which the heavens in cloudless lustre smil'd,
Where proudly Nature's primal charms appear'd,
Might well a heart less sad than hers have cheer'd;
And there, but few moons past, Menana stood,
To gaze upon that variegated flood,
With that emotion, scarce to be defin'd,
That sometimes steals upon the musing mind,
A pensive feeling, neither grave nor gay,
Calm as the twilight of a summer's day.
Again she stood there; but how different now
The consciousness that sat upon her brow!
The scene, though still the same, had lost its spell,
*One* thought was in her breast sole sentinel.
Ah! could she now behold, in earth or sky,
Aught to assure her that *he* should not die?
Nor earth, nor sky, one ray of hope could yield;
The hours were fleeting, and his fate was seal'd.

   " Why, ye small timid tenants of the air,
" Seek," she commun'd, " the wily serpent's glare?
" Why drop beneath his fascinating glance,
" As if subjected to some fatal trance?
" But are not men, too, of the serpent kind?
" Have *they* no venom?   Coil *they* not and wind?

" The stronger make the weaker still their prey,
" With force destroy, or with a smile betray!
" Oh, that our warlike tribes, alike in hue,
" Alike in valour, were in love as true!
" That they in peaceful brotherhood might live,
" Forget their feuds and mutually *forgive!* "

Thus mus'd Menana, when, as if a light,
New born of Heaven, had burst upon her sight.
She now devoutly rais'd a cross of gold,
Till then conceal'd within her vestment's fold,
Which still her mother's memory renew'd,
While many a heartfelt tear her eyes bedew'd :
That cross, of Hope, Faith, Charity, the sign,
Eternal emblem of a grace divine!
Menana's! How, in that rude heathen land,
Became it hers? Could *she* then understand
The Christian's creed? Or know what holy charm
Belong'd to that bright relic? Could she arm
Her soul with trust and confidence in HIM,
Whose throne is fix'd above the Cherubim ?

Menana had been taught, in early youth,
To know the SAVIOUR and revere the truth ;
No Indian maiden born : long years had past
Since on that Western coast a wreck was cast ;
Many there were on board, but few with life
Escap'd that scene of elemental strife.

Amongst the last, a mother and her child,
A little daughter who look'd up and smil'd;
It was Menana in life's sweetest stage,
Ere grief had sadden'd nature's buoyant age;
When her young soul had just began to beam,
Like dawning light upon a crystal stream;
And every charm of innocence and truth
Promis'd to ripen into blushing youth.
Such was Menana then. Who view'd her now,
Saw modest dignity upon her brow;
Than this none further sought or wish'd to scan,
But deem'd her daughter of brave Simaghan.
A third, a man of piety and years,
Whose mission was to dry the sinner's tears,
Was also sav'd; but soon he stray'd alone,
Few heeded whither, and to all unknown.

But whence that wreck, whose fragments scatter'd lay
Deeply imbedded in yon distant bay?[a]
Its nation, name, none, save Menana, knew;
And over these a constant veil she drew;
But even she had little to disclose,
That told of others' perils or their woes;
Yet still she felt a clasping mother's kiss,
Amidst that night's too horrible abyss,

---

[a] This passage alludes to a fact recorded in the history of Louisiana, from which it appears that the sea had receded considerably from the land.

Warm on her cheek; remember'd still a pray'r
That Heaven her guileless little one would spare;
And with what earnest hands that mother press'd
The sacred cross upon her infant's breast;
Where it had since like hidden wealth remain'd,
By no rude eye or ruder hand profan'd.
'Twas now that holy crucifix once more
Reviv'd a feeling she had known before,
But which, uncherish'd 'mid unchristian sway,
Had slept, but had not wholly died away.
She bow'd her head and bent her knee in pray'r,
With contrite spirit, like a statue there;
And when she rose, by all save One unseen,
Her step was steady and her look serene;
Yet on her brow appear'd some firm resolve,
Whatever danger it might chance involve,
And hope again a gleam of lustre shed,
As to a secret shady creek she sped.
   In that secluded nook, a small canoe
Securely lay conceal'd from strangers' view;
A fragile bark, but one that oft had borne,
At eventide or at the blush of morn,
Its sylph-like owner, led by choice or chance,
Amidst those golden realms of rude romance,
To seize an hour of rapture all her own,
And contemplate the works of God alone.
When rose the full-orb'd moon in silvery pride,
Reflected in the Mississippi's tide;

And myriad stars, her radiant handmaids, shone
Through all the concave of her azure-throne,
Then would Menana, in her birch-bark boat,
O'er the broad belt of mighty waters float,
And through those depths that weaker minds would
   scare,
Oft pause awhile to view its image there,
As if suspended in pellucid air.
Sometimes, beneath the bright transparent wave,
She'd gaze far down on some vast, stony cave;
Where, too, all wild stupendous forms arose,
Gigantic crags and rocks in deep repose,
By some convulsive shock together hurl'd,
Like riven fragments of a former world,
A world of which huge creatures, now unknown,
Have left but limbs of skeletons alone.[a]
Then would she ply again the plashing oar,
Fearless as free, and skirt along the shore.
With anxious step to seek that skiff she hied,
And stores within it secretly provide;
Weapons and food she thither bore, as bent
On working out some well-contriv'd intent;
Nor for herself alone appear'd her care,
Some other one had in her thoughts a share:
But soon, with cautious art, she saw elate
The slender vessel bear its needful freight;

---

[a] The mammoth. See *North American Rambler.*

And, in the shade of night, unflinching, brave,
As if she had been the spirit of the wave,
She floated noiseless in her stor'd canoe,
Till to the next encampment near she drew.

One more day's route before the war-host lay,
And now again they speeded on their way;
But one bright morning's sun again would rise,
Ere they would reach the place of sacrifice.
That distance gain'd, the usual halt was made,
And on the sward their weary limbs were laid.
The death-song now the fated captive sung,
Amus'd the elder, but inflam'd the young;
Yet still some chance remain'd, dissentions rose,
Not all were merciless, though all his foes;
A special council hence was call'd, to take
The general voice for slavery or the stake.

**END OF CANTO THE SECOND.**

# MENANA.

---

## CANTO III.

---

" Ambition this shall tempt to rise;
    Then whirl the wretch from high,
To bitter scorn a sacrifice,
    And grinning infamy."—GRAY.

---

DEEP in a glen, a wild and woody tract,
Far from the roaring of the cataract,
Large cypress-branches form'd the senate-dome,
Whose ample shadow spread a solemn gloom.
The owl sat moping on the wither'd limb
Of an old oak, conceal'd in covert dim.
Through neighbouring groves the soft, cool, sighing
        breeze
Fann'd the high nests embower'd among the trees;
And 'midst the foliage swarms of fire-flies shone,
Like tiny stars, spangling an earthly throne;

For night approach'd, and light clouds flitted by,
The fleecy graces of a summer's sky.
The council-grove a fire's red glare display'd,
And each swarth face grew swarthier in its shade.
There Simaghan, the Senior-Sachem, wore
The insignia of the potent sway he bore.
Around him fifty elders, richly clad
In beaver-skins, all seeming grave, if glad,
Assembled now to hold their last debate;
A few to mercy mov'd, but more to hate.
Some chiefs were tattoo'd[a] o'er with figures quaint,
Or rude device, in various colour'd paint.
These had the tortoise, fox, or serpent trac'd;
The bear, or beaver, those, on breast and waist.
Below the girth a robe was drawn around,
By shells or beads in graceful fillets bound;
Or locks of hair, the juice of flowers had dyed,
Compos'd a fringe in rude fantastic pride.
Thus, in the lurid shade, half gleam, half gloom,
They sat to fix the captive's final doom.
Such was the place and such the council, where
The Natchez Chief was summon'd to repair;
His name resounded through the foliag'd roof,
With yells of joy, of conscious triumph proof;
Of triumph over one whose proudest claim
Had been to foil them in their warlike aim;

---

[a] Tattooing is only occasionally practised among the North
American Indians; the custom is not universal.

Whose prowess oft had sham'd their utmost might,
And put the boldest of their chiefs to flight;
Whose skill had baffled many a subtle snare
To seize him or destroy.   He now was there.
Soon as the elders silence could impose,
With stately mien wise Simaghan arose.
His presence spread a general awe around,
Alike for arms and policy renown'd.
But brief the pause ; the silence thus he broke,
As to the chief the aged warrior spoke :

"For death prepare ! thy sentence is decreed !
"No friendly voice hath deign'd for thee to plead.
" But three moons since thou wert condemn'd before,
" When we were slow to look upon thy gore ;
" Perchance we took compassion on thy youth,
" And woman's weakness turn'd our hearts to ruth.
" But now no pity can thy days prolong
" Beyond the morrow's sun ; in all this throng
" No glance of mercy beams to mitigate
" The taunts and tortures that upon thee wait.
" Yet would we thou didst still some hope retain
" To burst thy shackles and be free again,
" That disappointment might increase thy pain ;
" Since thou didst once our careless grasp-elude,
" And now art sprinkled with our kinsman's blood.
" We found his lone canoe upon the sand,
" The polish'd paddles plac'd to meet his hand ;

" Upon the sedgy bank some chance had thrown
' The moose-hide targe and quiver once his own.
" Whose arm had plung'd him in an early grave,
" Thou best canst tell—he slept beneath the wave.
" We found the body, but the life was fled,
" And thou wert there exulting o'er the dead.
" For death prepare ! the flames will shortly rise,
" To wrap thee in thy deep-wrung agonies ;
" Yet still this tribute to thy tribe we owe,
" Thy last expiring pangs shall be but *slow ;*
" And if thou'rt worthy of thy name and race,
" Thou wilt not either in that hour disgrace.
" Vengeance through all our woody echoes cries !"


" Then why delay the wish'd-for sacrifice?
" Here stands your self-confest, your deadliest foe ;
" 'Twas this bare arm that struck your idol low ;
" I own the deed, would 'twere to do again !
" But listen ! though you'll hear me not complain :
" Yes, you have said aright ; I once before
" Was doom'd to glut your vengeance with my gore.
" Look on these wounds ; they seem almost as fresh
" As when your flint-barb'd arrows pierc'd the flesh ;
" These many scars with lighted splinters try,
" And mark how well they shall your rage defy ;
" Or probe them as ye will, revenge to sate,
" And rouse your malice into deadlier hate.

" But still ye shall in vain attempt to wring
" A groan, despite of mortal quivering.
" My soul shall never be by pain subdu'd,
" But bear erect its native attitude.
" Low burnt your watch-fires, and their flickering ray
" Shew'd where your chiefs on wicker hurdles<sub>a</sub> lay ;
" One only guard the smoking-weed<sup>b</sup> retain'd,
" And his the only eye unclos'd remain'd.
" Midnight had pass'd, till then the moon's pale light
" Had been conceal'd from my impatient sight.
" The unfolding night-plant breath'd its sweetest balm,
" The sky was placid and the air was calm ;
" Nor did an oar upon the shadowy lake
" The stillness of the dew-ey'd morning break.
" 'Twas then I burst my bonds, no matter how,
" And left your guards to brook your angry brow.
" Since then I might of other exploits tell,
" But some among your matrons know them well.
" Let this suffice : as in the shade I lay,
" Weary, alone, upon the close of day,
" With stealthy footsteps came a secret foe,
" And o'er my head was rais'd the fatal blow ;
" Another moment, and his cunning might
" Have now prevented this too tedious rite ;

---

<sup>a</sup> " They lie before the fire on hurdles of reeds, covered with a mat, sometimes with skins."—*Pinkerton's Voyages.*
<sup>b</sup> Tobacco.

" When with a sudden spring I turn'd aside
" The uplifted arm, I cleft him and he died!
" That foe was he you now deplore in vain,
" The lurking coward by my hatchet slain.
" Short was the struggle; in the wave his corse
" I threw, and would again without remorse.—
" You know the rest."

      " We do!" cried Simaghan,
" That deed we own might have become a man.
" Once more escape! will the fierce Cougar e'er
" Let free his prey, if once within his lair?
" Then if again thy limbs be ever freed,
" Deride us for our vigilance indeed!
" Who taught thee, save some old decrepit squaw,
" To poise the spear or childhood's bow to draw?
" Perchance, thou hast among thy mates been found
" To boast a scratch, pretending it a wound.
" The 'Pale Face' prattles, but is not believ'd,
" Nor thou proclaiming wounds in war receiv'd.
" Of little maims the brave disdain to speak;
" Such boasts befit alone the puny weak."

The youthful warrior, with indignant look,
Thus answer'd to the sneer he could not brook :
" Unwelcome words like mine excite your ire,
" As stagnant pools, disturb'd, cast up their mire.
" But the Good Spirit bids us truth declare,
" And from a hollow specious lie forbear.

" Is there a warrior's or a hunter's name
" That fork-tongu'd falsehood ever rais'd to fame ?
" Sooner the yellow-tassell'd maize, in sooth,
" For him will ripen who but speaks the truth ;
" For him the smoking-leaf will grow with speed,
" But worms[a] consume his lying neighbour's weed ;
" Whoever heard that deer or moose were found
" Within the boastful liar's hunting-ground ?
" Whoever knew him triumph o'er a foe,
" But he was soon in combat sunk as low ?
" 'Tis truth I speak ! I look not down, mine eye
" Can meet the Great Good Spirit's scrutiny :
" No skins can hide us from HIS searching view ;
" I boast not, lie not, all my words are true !"

" It may be so, but of thy vaunts beware ! "
(Rejoin'd the Sachem, with an angry glare.)
" Would'st seek to snatch its cubling from the bear ?
" Or meet the gaunt wolf raging for his prey ?
" Soon for such fool-like rashness would'st thou pay :
" Here, too, thy words are as the onward wind,
" That leaves no sound of blustering breath behind.
" To-morrow thou shalt die ! the morning's light
" Shall on thee close in one black, endless night !
" Thy death-chant vainly to the air thou'lt give ;
" Thy branded name shall scarce thyself outlive ;

---

[a] The green tobacco caterpillars.

" Lost to thy race, thy battle-feats shall raise
" No song of triumph and no shout of praise."

Now flash'd Tekarrah's eye with fearless pride,
As thus he unto Simaghan replied:—
" Ne'er shall my name be lost while grass grows green,
" Or mighty rivers flow their banks between;
" My father was the eagle of his tribe,
" And I have heard our aged chiefs describe
" His warlike deeds; his spirit breathes in me,
" Nor will I shame my father's memory!
" For he has fled to regions of the sun,
" The happy hunting-grounds our race hath won;
" Where now, methinks, my raptur'd eyes behold
" Those holy portals of pure molten gold,
" Which open to us that eternal state,
" The land of souls, the spirits of the great;
" Islands of light, that, in the Western sky,
" Are but reserv'd for those who bravely die.
" There thou shalt never mingle with the blest,
" 'Midst prairies with perennial verdure dress'd.—
" His trail was viewless and his foot was fleet,
" Too swift for foes to gain a safe retreat;
" Against the falls he steer'd his firm canoe,
" Or swam with ease the foaming torrent through;
" With twanging jerk the deadly shaft he sent
" From his tough bow with bison-sinews bent.
" In the hot strife, arm'd with the axe or lance,
" Terror with him was foremost to advance.

" Chief of the Eagle Plume ! his manly brow
" Ne'er bent before a foe, nor will *I* now.
" To him you bow'd your necks—forget it not !
" When will you clear away the branded blot ?—
" Whence Meschacebé[a], at its distant source,
" Sends forth its stream in one long devious course,
" Till where a thousand ceaseless currents blend
" In its broad bosom, widening as they bend ;
" Or rolling on, through wilds remote, to take
" Its gathering waters to the *Mighty Lake*[b]—
" My father made ye quail in every limb,
" Nor shall Tekarrah prove unworthy him.
" Yes, like my sire, your captive is not one
" To crave your mercy, or your vengeance shun.
" Behold me, like my race, as firm as brave ;
" Nor, if ye spar'd me, would I live your slave.
" *I* never from ye shrunk in battle's rage,
" *I* never fear'd the fiercest to engage.
" Though in your war-pole feats[c] ye vaunt your might,
" Warriors but mock your prowess in the fight ;
" Squaws are not men, and squaws your warriors are,
" Who every where are warriors but in war !"

　　The Sachem curl'd his lip :—" Cease, daring boy !
" Nor in such ravings thus thy time employ ;

---

　　　　[a] Mississippi.　　　　　[b] The ocean.
　　[c] Sham exploits.　See *History of Louisiana*, p. 372.

" Think not to swerve us by such idle theme,
" Heeded no more than is the fitful gleam
" Of summer lightning in an evening sky,
" That augurs heat, but passes harmless by.
" Thou boast'st of skill in war, contempt of fear—
" Why have we then the Natchez-leader here?
" Thou'rt like the Rattle-snake, whose noisy trail
" Gives ample note to those he would assail;
" But the black serpent softly steals, unheard,
" Till, with one spring, he strikes his victim-bird.
" Thy fruitless pride this vain delirium feeds;
" We teach *our* youth to practice only deeds.
" A chief is known by acts, not sounding talk;
" He wields no weapon but the tomahawk.
" The tongue's *thy* weapon, us'd by thee not least;
" Preaching is but the province of the priest[a].
" When words are many, deeds are oft but scant,
" As trees in leaves abound, in fruit they want[b];
" Nay, frown not, babbler! thou hast yet to learn,
" A captive's looks are not so very stern.

---

[a] Some of the native tribes, as the Natchez, were not without ministers of religion, who acknowledged a Supreme Being, and may not improperly be denominated priests. They had, however, a secular as well as a sacred office; and, being skilled in the art of medicine, were therefore more often called *Medicine-Men*.

[b] After writing the couplet in the text, I was somewhat startled on finding the same idea expressed in *Pope's Essay on Criticism*.

"Though eagles on the smaller birds will swoop,
" I will not deign for timid prey to stoop ;
" Nor is my wont to treat my foes with scorn ;
" Let him act basely who is basely born !
" Captive ! bewail thy birth and destiny ;
" Sleep if thou canst awhile, at morn to die !"


" Sachem ! behold me as if once more freed,
" No crouching coward, and no bending reed !
" Why not at once prepare your pompous pile ?
" Will it extort a groan ? it may a smile ;
" And when your eager flames this form embrace,
" Mark then if terror in my soul have place.
" Haply with you sharp pain produces tears,
" The Natchez warriors know no childish fears.
" Your strength in fight and firmness to endure
" Are balanc'd by revenge and crafty lure ;
" But brave example shows what men may do
" Without unworthy pains to make them true.
" I've cleft the wicker casque from many a brow,
" And left the wearers in the dust below ;
' I've drawn my arrow to its feathery head,
" Till through my foe it pass'd out reeking red.
" Then cease to menace, let me burn or bleed,
" Great Manitou to bright abodes will lead ;
" Commence your work, nor waste your time for me ;
" You bind my body, but my soul is free.

" Mine be the meed, for mine shall be the pride
" Of bravely dying as my fathers died !"

His hearers' eyes flash'd fire, their tongues were
  mute,
And Simaghan no longer held dispute;
But, 'midst the council, on a tall tree's bough,
An Indian sat, with dark and sullen brow;
Silent he bent, then suddenly address'd
A light-wing'd arrow to Tekarrah's breast.
Though with precision aim'd, the shaft mis-sped,
But pierc'd the hero's arm, which freely bled.
Yet scarce had ceas'd the twanging bow its sound,
Ere he resum'd, and smil'd upon the wound.

" Dastard ! full oft the forest tree receives
" And hides a lurking laggard by its leaves;
" Your skulking form thick branches ill conceal,
" You have a woman's heart, but mine is steel.
" Curl not your lip in scorn, I dare defy
" And mock the rage that kindles in your eye.
" The wren can bluster ᵃ in his little might,
" The prairie-dog will bark, but seldom bite;
" A breath will make the coward shrink with fear,
" As rustling fern alarms the timid deer.

---

[a] The wren is called by the French, in derision, *Roitelet* (Petty
King).—*Du Pratz.*

"The roar of thunder and the lightning's flash
"Would make you tremble and your souls abash;
"At our war-whoop with nimble feet ye fly,
"And dread the arrow's point,—afraid to die;
"Your courage dares not meet an equal foe,
"Your shafts are feeble and their flight is slow;
"In ambush skulk you not, like owls at night?
"The brave despise such craven modes of fight.
"How weak your arm! how powerless to mine!
"A reed compar'd to some proud towering pine!"

Meanwhile, the victim of their ruthless strife,
To linger out another night of life—
But that the last—was thence securely led,
On the green sward once more to lay his head;
That rest and slumber might his frame prepare
To meet the horrors it was doom'd to bear.
Now, by their past experience wiser grown,
They trusted to no single guard alone;
But six they chose, the wariest of their tribe,
Deem'd to be proof against deceit or bribe;
They from the Sachem's lips their charge receiv'd,
Strictly to watch, but soon to be reliev'd;
Others, as wary, should in turn succeed,
Thus to be ready for the morning's deed.

How quick, how fertile, too, is woman's brain!
The words Menana caught, nor caught in vain;

Nought to her hopes could more propitious be,
Could she rely on faith and secrecy.
'Tis midnight, and above the tranquil scene
The stars shine forth as radiant as serene;
A witching stillness o'er the landscape creeps,
And all but anxious love in soundness sleeps.
The lake is dimpled by the balmy breeze,
Fraught with the fragrance of the wild lime-trees;
And, on its surface calmly slumbering,
The water-bird now rests its weary wing;
Now, peaceful flows the Mississippi's tide,
As if the moon had bade it smoothly glide,
Lest e'en its murmurs might awake the flow'rs
Reposing sweetly in their leafy bow'rs.
Nought breaks the silence, save the lonely sound
Of the far waterfalls; the woods around
Wave not aloft their proudly towering crest;
But water, earth, and sky, are all at rest,
Or listening but to hear the mellow thrill,
The plaintive carol of the Whip-poor-Will[a].

The Sachem, now on his rush-mat reclin'd,
Would fain forget the cares that goad his mind;
His weary eyes unwelcome vigils keep,
For feverish thoughts prevent his wonted sleep.

---

[a] *Caprimulgus minor Americanus.* The Indian name for this bird is *Wekolis.*

Dim wasting hiccory-torches near him glow,
But there is on his heart a weight of woe.
'Tis strange, Menana nowhere can be found,
And all the woods and wilds her name resound ;
Scouts are despatch'd to seek her far and near ;
But all alike return with looks of fear.
They deem some sudden ill must have betray'd,
But what they cannot guess, the absent maid ;
And Simaghan, by strong emotions vex'd,
Pines the long night, with various thoughts perplex'd;
While poor Menana's wilder'd mind is bent
On objects distant from the Sachem's tent.


Perforce, within the maiden's bosom grew
A secret passion, guess'd but by the few,
To none reveal'd—a feeling cherish'd long,
Before she knew 'twas love, or deem'd 'twas wrong :
Like some remembrances of former years,
That blanch the cheek and fill the eye with tears;
Some check'd emotion, or some wish represt,
Some modest thought shrin'd in a virgin breast,
Some patient suffering, or some lurking grief,
A canker-worm within the rose-bud's leaf.
But from her lips unconsciously would fall
Words, if she knew them, she would fain recall.
Oh! 'twas a vow! an oath in heaven repos'd,
And to no mortal ear to be disclos'd,

That she would ne'er her early faith forsake,
For all that earth could give or heaven could take:
*Never with infidel to wed,* nor e'er
Forget her mother's last, fond, dying pray'r—
To live an exile and a virgin, till
God should restore her, by His gracious will,
To Christian climes, perchance her native land,
Conducted by His all-paternal hand.
Oppressive thus e'en love's sweet bonds became,
Since they inflicted but a sense of shame,
Of anguish, overwhelming to the heart
That bade for love pure piety depart;
And now she felt that speechless, deep distress,
Earth might increase, but Heaven alone make less.
But when she saw Tekarrah's youthful frame
In fancy tortur'd by the circling flame,
Her love, resistless, threw each barrier down,
To save his life or with it lose her own.
Then straight she hasten'd to complete her plan,
While time was ripe, unknown to Simaghan.

### END OF CANTO THE THIRD.

# MENANA.

---

## CANTO IV.

---

"This is your hour, and best you may command."
*Robert Herrick's Hesperides.*

THE Sachem's numerous host, the guard except,
In hut, or pirogue unsuspecting slept.
Who of the chief's escape could harbour fear?
Too strong their camp for foes to venture near.
His hands and feet were fasten'd to a tree;
But nought disturb'd his soul's serenity.
With fortitude resolv'd to meet his fate,
He thus soliloquis'd his wretched state,
While at short distances upon the ground
The sentries slept, or seem'd to sleep, around.

"Asleep! my guards! your vigils soon are done;
"Then slumber on, and dream till rise of sun.
"Quickly, it seems, your faithful trust is o'er;
"The watcher's watch'd, the watch'd is watch'd no
more.

" A few brief hours, and whither shall I be ?

" Why wish for life ?   Why envy now the free ?

" I crave no mercy, none they had from me.

" When the gaunt wolf the dappled doe has found,

" Leaves he it gor'd and bleeding on the ground ?

" Ah, no ! its gaping wounds but more excite

" The raging fierceness of his appetite.

" Then why should I my adverse fate repine ?

" As theirs is now, the wilderness *was* mine,

" And may be mine again, if Manitou

" But interpose, and if my dreams be true.

" Faint heart and failing knees at home should stay,

" And join with children in their puerile play ;

" Who dares not bend the bow in fight, should coop

" With timid squaws, and shun the fierce war-whoop.

" Let the poor trapper in his hut remain,

" To spin the thread of all his days in vain ;

" String wampum-shells, or gather nuts and fruits,

" Or mix with women in their weak pursuits ;

" Or on some rock, if in a venturous mood,

" With tender hand hook up the speckled brood ;

" Mark the leaf fall, the prairie-grass grow sere,

" Ensnare the bird, or track the harmless deer.

" No ! rather let me prove my own true friend,

" And from this earth my prison-tree uprend ;

" And when its prostrate trunk shall lie at length,

" Anew they'll marvel at Tekarrah's strength.

" Ne'er shall they gaze upon my livid cheek,

" Nor on my bones shall vultures whet their beak ;

" Nor will I creep through hazels, like the snake,
" But my bold way along the war-path take.
" While now these sentinels around me lie,
" What if my courage and this arm I try !
" Oh, then could I, to give my foes no clue,
" My flying footsteps with dry leaves bestrew ;
" Or, lest my mocassins should mark my track,
" Lay lightly e'en the tell-tale grass-blades back ;
" Thus foil pursuit, and like an arrow flee—
" So they who deem'd me bound, might seek me free.
" Great Manitou ! oh, hear my prayers, and keep
" Awhile these watch-dogs in their heavy sleep ;
" Grant now thine aid, the tempting time invites,
" And yet preserve me for a hundred fights ;
" Speed my light steps, until my native plain
" Once more I tread, with warriors in my train !"

  As for his flight the Eagle spreads his wings,
Or from his lair the hungry panther springs,
So was Tekarrah ready to extend
His utmost strength and quick his bondage end ;
When, lo ! his guards upsprang, as from a trance,
And pointed at his breast the deadly lance.
A smile of malice on their features play'd,
And mock'd his hopes thus bitterly betray'd.
Slumber they had but feign'd ; too well they knew
What, if their charge escap'd, themselves would rue ;
Nor had they aught of feeling that responds
To sympathy that shares the captive's bonds.

Dismay'd, he sunk, but unreveal'd his grief,
Though hopeless now all prospect of relief.
Again his guards compos'd themselves to rest,
But, steps advancing, near the chief they press'd;
Cautious, they look'd around with curious eye—
Others had come their places to supply.
Few words exchang'd, the former watch withdrew,
The last seem'd scarce to keep their charge in view.

But see! what light and lovely form appears
Like a bright star descended from the spheres!
Nearer she comes—Menana! and alone!
But to herself her purpose only known.
She moves; but with a slow and noiseless tread;
And not a leaf is stirr'd above her head.
Tekarrah sees along the moonlight glade
The maid approach, like some angelic shade;
While she, by gestures, which he soon descries,
Warns him to give no token of surprise.
Oh, ask not why her mossy couch she leaves,
Nor what her eyes of gentle sleep bereaves;
She comes to set the captive chieftain free—
Oh, Love! what will not Beauty do for thee?
She comes, like one subdu'd in soul and tone,
Whose hope for ever from this world is gone;
But with an elevated mien and air
That shows a mind superior to despair.
She comes, life, freedom, rapture, to dispense,
But dead herself to every joyous sense.

With maiden blushes and with timid haste,
She drew a polish'd weapon from her waist;
Then quickly cut the captive's bonds in twain—
Tekarrah stood in freedom once again.
Yet now so potent were the spells of love,
He seem'd transfix'd, nor had the power to move.
Upon the maid he gaz'd with burthen'd heart,
But wanted words his feelings to impart;
'Till, as she now retreated from his reach,
He thus address'd the maid in gentle speech:

" Dove of the Forest! wilt thou stay not near?
" Sweet Woodland Flower! oh, do not harbour fear!
" No lurking danger here shall do thee harm;
" Or should it threaten, wear'st thou not a charm
" Of beauty, that would every evil chase
" From the bright presence of thy heavenly face?"

Menana shrunk, for now she saw that gore
Was flowing from his wounded arm, and tore
Her veil with which she papwa-leaves[a] applied;
And with her hair the healing balsam tied.
She then, with tears, invok'd no longer stay,
As thus she urg'd him on his destin'd way.

" Chief of a hostile nation! hear my voice!
" Thou shalt not perish yet; in that rejoice!

---

[a] Annona triloba.

" Return thee to thy huts and native plains,
" No foe prevents thee, and no bond restrains."

Mutely he stood; though few her words, their tone
Chang'd him as if he had insensate grown ;
Depriv'd he seem'd of all the powers of mind,
As lightning strikes the fated vision blind.
While thus entranc'd, she motion'd him along,
From instant danger and the sleeping throng ;
Her bosom heav'd, her cheek betray'd a blush,
Pale grew her lips, and tears began to gush ;
As light showers oft succeed the breath of morn,
So flow'd her tears of orient blushes born.
Again she spoke, and thus her accents fell
Soft on his ear, like some supernal spell.

" Must I entreat thee ? must I sue in vain ?
" The moments seize that will not come again.
" Thy guards are safe, they sleep,—I did bethink
" To mix an opiate in their evening drink ;
" Snatch, then, the precious instant, and be free
" As forest bird, and end my misery !
" Cast not thyself upon the Jaguar's path,
" The mangled prey of fierce and famish'd wrath.
" Compel me not to know thy cruel death,
" To see thee yield thy faint expiring breath ;
" To hear the name thy foes pronounc'd with fear
" Become a by-word for their children's jeer ;

" Once more by flight defeat thine enemies,

" And, eagle-like, regain thy native skies;

" Would the poor leagur'd stag so patient be,

" Could he o'erleap his danger and be free?

" Freedom invites, all barriers are withdrawn,

" Haste, haste away, nor wait the fatal dawn.

" Means thou wilt find to baffle every foe

" With these sharp arrows and this trusty bow;

" Take them; but if their crystal points be seen

" In the moon's ray, thine enemies are keen

" Of sight as the jet snake—they might betray—

" Speed, then, and leave no trail upon thy way.

" Fly to the westward, follow yonder star,

" And it will guide thee to a creek—not far—

" Where thou wilt find a little bark-built shell,

" My own canoe; and now a last farewell!

" The red man's boon upon thy steps attend,

" The bow, the beaver-cloak, the faithful friend.

" But, hark! that sound!   Methought the bushes
            stirr'd—

" What! if perchance we now were overheard?

" Oh, could'st thou then successfully oppose

" Thy single breast against a host of foes?

" Soon will they miss thee, soon each track pursue,

" Wind every wood and follow every clue—

" Ah! what but speed can save thee then, or *who?*

" No spot can screen thee, if thou lingerest nigh;

" Nor bank, nor rock, nor cave, nor covert high.

" Go, thread the forest, shun the treacherous light,
" And gain the mountains by the aid of night.
" Once more I urge thee to depart, and leave
" Menana in her loneliness to grieve ;
" Or soon thy foes will all thy steps enthral,
" Numerous as squirrels where the beech-nuts fall.
" When once again thou minglest with thy kind,
" My image soon will vanish from thy mind ;
" Forget the past, since I no more can be
" Than now I am to thee, or thou to me.
" Go, choose some maiden of a kindred race,
" Whose charms will every thought of me efface ;
" One fit to make a happier bride than I,
" Whose only fate is—to despair and die !
" Oh, let me urge thee once again, depart—
" Yet take this token of a faithful heart ;
" These cherish'd beads around thy neck suspend [a] ;
" It may sometimes remind thee of a friend ;
" Then deem that friend as one of life bereft,
" Or scarcely with a sense of being left ;
" Think of her like a dream for ever fled—
" The giver but remember'd with the dead.
" But I forget myself—o'er furze and fell
" God speed thy moccasins ! farewell ! farewell !"
Then from her hair she took a jasmine wreath,
And with it crown'd his brows—for life, not death.

---

[a] Her rosary

" Oh, woman ! loveliest of created things !
" Thy sympathy can ease the sharpest stings,
" Thy tenderness can solace sweet instil,
" And, oh ! thy love's a balm for every ill.
" Dear ministress of good to all around,
" With gentle grace and heavenly beauty crown'd ;
" How prompt to succour with unsought relief,
" How patient under suffering and grief !
" Meek, soothing, tender, breathing looks benign,
" Human in form, but, oh ! in soul divine !"
Such glowing sentiments inspir'd his mind,
Till thus again his thoughts could utterance find.


" Child of my *foe*, for thee I aught would dare,
" For thee would all thy nation's vengeance bear ;
" Ere I had known thee, would that I had died—
" Methinks I see thee now another's bride !
" Or is the white-rose maiden's heart too small
" The love of two ' *red-faces* ' to enthral ?
" Ah, no ! e'en now these aching eyes behold
" Some happier rival all thy charms enfold ;
" I see thy careful hands arrange his dress ;
" Thy lips to his with fervent ardour press,
" Or, while he mingles in the Green-Corn dance,
" Mark thee regard him with admiring glance.
" Now dost thou bind his brow with fragrant flow'rs,
" Or waste in amorous dalliance idle hours ;

" Now for his downy couch, with anxious care,
" The cypress-moss thy willing hands prepare;
" And, as from hunting toils outstretch'd he lies,
" Thou watchest o'er him till sleep close his eyes.
" Or stain'st his forehead red with paint [a] of wrath,
" To daunt his foes upon the battle-path.
" Some rival will deprive my heart of rest,
" And steal thee, pretty eaglet, from thy nest!
" Few moons have circled, love, since first we met,
" And think'st thou that I can so soon forget
" The tender looks thou gav'st me then, the words
" Breath'd from thy lips, like melody of birds?
" As yon clear orb shines through the boughs above,
" So the GOOD SPIRIT beam'd upon our love;
" Thy smile to me in that sweet hour was bliss,
" I deem'd it mutual—Oh! what change is this?
" What though new life thou dost on me bestow,
" Life, without thee, were only ceaseless woe!
" Am I not calm? this heart no fear can whelm;
" It trembles not, no more than yonder elm.
" Yet ere I now thy lovely form beheld,
" I felt my soul too mighty to be quell'd:
" Methought the spirits of my sires look'd down [b],
" And on my tame submission seem'd to frown.

---

[a] Vermilion.

[b] The North American Indians cherish a superstition that certain places are haunted by spirits, whose power they dread; for which reason they cautiously shun the places which they are supposed to frequent.

" Rather than brook their stern, imperious scorn,
"These sturdy trees I would have fain uptorn ;
" The love of life, of liberty, return'd,
" But what are they, if I by thee am spurn'd ?
"Thou weep'st ! dim not those lotus-eyes with grief,
" White-bosom'd daughter of a victor-chief !
"Thou bid'st me flee, would'st have me swift depart ?
" Giv'st freedom to my limbs, but not my heart ?
" As well command me, stretch'd on frozen plains,
"To feel a genial warmth within my veins,
" Or hope to find a summer shadow trac'd
" On the bright lake by winter uneffac'd.
"Escape !   Oh ! 'twere an easy task indeed ;
" Swift as a four-moons' fawn should be my speed ;
" Or, I would, like the hunted moose-deer, hide
"Beneath some lake[a], and keenest search deride ;
" Or, like the finny tribe, with sleepless eye[b],
" For danger watch, and then from danger fly.
"Though not with weapons of white men supplied,
"The fiery tube and death-balls at my side,
" No stout canoe to stem the rapid's force,
" Nor e'en thy bow and arrows, no resource,

---

[a] There is a prevalent opinion, that among other means of self-preservation employed by the moose, and in which this animal excels beyond most others, one is its capability of remaining for a long time under water.  For a curious account on this subject, see *Tanner's Narrative.*

[b] It is said that fish never sleep, having no eye-lids, nor any membrane to cover the visual organ, as all other animals have.

" Save in my own fleet foot and strength of arm,
" Still I should bear a more than mystic charm,
" Come peril in whatever shape it might,
" If thou would'st be companion in my flight.
" If not, farewell to all my soul's desire,
" And let me at thy feet at once expire !"


Menana linger'd, yet was loth to stay,
Afraid her heart it's weakness should betray.
It did betray—few can their steps retrace,
When what they most should shun they half embrace.
Receding now, and now inclin'd to share
Her lover's flight and every danger dare.
She paus'd, and then her mind instinctive cast
A hurried glance at youth and childhood past ;
Next would Tekarrah's peril flash to view,
With all the horrors that too well she knew.
The future could not darker be than this,
And hope array'd it in the hues of bliss.
And now she sigh'd, as in her thought arose
The friends whose care had banish'd early woes ;
To leave the sire whose hand had led her own,
Since she from helpless infancy had grown,
And, oh ! to leave him without one farewell,
Awoke a pang she knew not how to quell.
How often had he listen'd to her song,
Which echo seem'd enraptur'd to prolong !

Should he then hear no more that gentle voice,
That soothed his cares and made his soul rejoice?
She deem'd the very buds that round her grew
Implor'd her stay with tears of scented dew;
Her wigwam-home, its flowers, its trees, its stream,
Floated in wilder'd fancy, like a dream,—
A thousand thoughts a moment will embrace,
And each the other in succession chase.
Thus mus'd the maid, the conflict in her breast
Held her as doubtful what resolve were best;
Timid her heart's fond dictates to obey,
Yet dreading if Tekarrah there should stay!
With his entreaty she at length complied,
Content for love to hazard all beside.
Eager he snatch'd, at once, the yielding maid,
And bore her swiftly through the favoring shade.
Few words sufficed to point his steps—he flew
To the small creek, where lay her stor'd canoe.

END OF CANTO THE FOURTH.

# MENANA.

## CANTO V.

" How cheerfully on the false trail they cry ! "

SHAKSPEARE.

" 'Tis far off,
" And rather like a dream than an assurance
" That my remembrance warrants."          IBID.

THE morn its way comes winging on the breeze,
'Midst sighs of odour from the spicy trees;
Night-clouds roll off apace, dun turns to grey,
The mist dispell'd, dawn dapples into day.
From Eastern realms the sun, in crimson glow,
Now tints with beauty half the world below;
From groves, and woods, and vales, sweet songs arise!
Upclimbs the lark with matin-hymn the skies,
As if ascending in a viewless car,
To sing blithe music to the morning star;
From nests in twisted roots or hollow tree,
The mottled[a] squirrel leaps right playfully;

---

[a] *Latrobe's Rambler in North America*, vol. ii, page 3.

Plants, fruits, and flowers disclose their richest hues,
Freshen'd and fragrant in the welcome dews;
The water-lily, 'midst its sombre leaves,
Its young and opening petals interweaves;
Fair fountains sparkle in their silvery sheen,
Through straggling alleys, or through vistas green;
Twice day and night had smoothly come and gone,
Since the two lovers had been hastening on;
Tekarrah, who each wise precaution knew,
Muffled the paddles of their light canoe.
The aspect of the sky wore not a frown,
And wild fowl on the current floated down.
With trusting heart Menana sat beside
Her all-devoted lover, guardian, guide;
Oft for his fond, assiduous care, the while
She well repaid him with her sweetest smile;
And oft she turn'd to view some woodland height,
As if recalling scenes of past delight;
The cheerful haunts of youthful, happy hours,
Her young companions and her favorite bowers;
Dear scenes of artless sport! where through the glades
Arose the laugh or song of Indian maids;
The waves that bore her gently on their breast,
As if obedient to her sweet behest;
Her reed-roof'd hut, by none unbidden trod,
Where she had oft alone commun'd with God;
But these she now had left, though long endear'd,
And Simaghan, still honor'd, still revered.

Yet scenes as fair now pass'd her anxious eye,
Where beauties seemed in endless range to lie;
Here, on the margin of a wandering stream,
Whose pearly shells shone in the sunny beam,
A thirsty fawn stood on a pendant bough,
To quaff the liquid element below,
While, near, the mock-bird warbled o'er her nest,
Lulling her unfledg'd offspring to their rest;
There islets, dazzling in the diamond dew,
Glisten'd, like stars, to charm the gazer's view;
While some in vestal chastity were dress'd,
With showers of snowy roses on their breast;
Others, like gorgeous dames, were proudly dight
In drapery rich and rainbow-colours bright;
Where from the water's edge encircling rose
Their vine-clad slopes, like graceful furbelows;
Whose little mounts, with spiral shrubs o'ergrown,
And crown'd with gaudy blossoms, formed a cone;
Round which the maiden-hair[a] dark grew beneath,
And tangled gold-thread[b] twin'd a silken wreath;
All seemed so many realms of fairy-land,
For Love created and by Beauty plann'd;
All sinless temples to great Nature's God,
For man had ne'er those grateful gardens trod;

---

[a] A species of fern, of the genus Adiantum.
[b] A small evergreen plant, *coptis trifolia*—so called from its fibrous, yellow roots.

Wild creatures, e'en that on each other prey'd,
There sought a truce to share the sun or shade :[a]
But none of all these charms her thoughts could wean
From what might be her lot, and what had been;
Nought from her heart oppression's weight remove,
Although that heart was flowing o'er with love.
Haply at intervals the calm around
Is broken by some intermittent sound;
The bison oft the foaming torrent dares,
Oppress'd beneath the weight of horns he bears;
With painful toil he plunges through the surf,
To gain some favorite copse, or mossy turf;
Where arbours, formed by nature, not by man,
Outspread their branches and project their span;
There, stretched along, he finds secure repose,
On the rich sward which e'er abundant grows,
Nor aught to human art or culture owes.
Oft would Tekarrah turn through distance dim,
To mark if foes were yet in quest of him;
Long had he seen their watch-fires brightly blaze,
And heard their shouts the forest echoes raise;
But Heaven the lovers' flight seemed now to guide,
By power unseen preserved on every side;

---

[a] These lines contain no exaggeration of the truth. It is an authenticated fact that animals, which have ordinarily the greatest antipathy towards each other, sometimes appear to forget all animosity, and share by a sort of tacit agreement in mutual enjoyment, whatever the occasion may present.

Love gave them wings, their bosoms hope inspired,
And from all danger they were far retired;
But if Menana slept awhile, he bent
His watchful ear, on every sound intent;
While, if at times he snatch'd a moment's rest,
She watch'd, as some fond bird her firstling's nest.

The distant hills at length appeared in sight,
To which Tekarrah pointed with delight;
But rush and reed impeded now their way,
And prairies near inclined them both to stay.
Close to the water's edge, a shelving lawn,
Where freely played the lightly bounding fawn,
With woods beyond, enticed them from their boat,
Which in a shallow creek they left to float.
" Beyond those lofty hills," Tekarrah cries,
" My native village, lov'd Menana! lies;
" Bosom'd in trees and safe from every foe,
" There we may all the sweets of union know;
" But now thou'rt weary, and at evening's close,
" As sets the sun, 'tis meet thou should'st repose
" In the thick covert of yon forest green,
" The branching boughs afford a leafy screen;
" There thou may'st refuge find from breeze and show'r;
" The festoon'd plant and scarlet-trailing flow'r
" Shall, wreathing round thee, form a curtain'd bow'r
" The oak's white moss shall be thy tranquil bed,
" And slumber o'er thy lids shall gently spread:

E

" There will I watch and guard thee from affright,
" Till fades the moon and dawns the morning light."

As a young flower with heavy dews o'erprest,
She bow'd her head upon her lover's breast,
While frequent blushes, mantling o'er her cheek,
Betray'd what her pure love forbade to speak;
But, oh! could he his boundless joy restrain?
His was a rapture unalloy'd by pain!

In the wild opening of a glen, o'ergrown
With trees and tangled shrubs, the sun went down,
There, as they stood and view'd it sink, it shed
Along the hills a fierce and glowing red;
Tinging the clouds in masses, shapeless, cleft,
Till gloom o'ershadow'd all the track it left.

The spot selected for Menana's rest,
Her little bark became her cradled nest.
Soon from the creek, in which it idly lay,
Tekarrah bore it to the woods away;
There to the sturdy boughs that overhung,
Tied it with ozier bands, and firmly slung;
To which the gentle maid alone withdrew,
And thus Tekarrah breath'd his night's adieu:

" May blissful visions hover in the air
" Which to thy couch shall balmy odour bear,

" Stolen from the perfumes of the rich spice-trees
" That freight with incense every passing breeze.
" Visions as blest as those which float around
" That wondrous fount by Spring[a] for ever crown'd;
" Where palsied limbs may find their strength renew'd,
" And hoary age be with fresh youth imbu'd ;
" Where sweet illusions fill the raptur'd brain,
" And ceaseless pleasure banish every pain !
" And when thy care is o'er, as soon 'twill be,
" Then will I bring thee every luxury ;
" Berries I'll cull thee from the woods around,
" And cluster'd fruit shall at our hands abound.
" I know the deer-path and each hidden track ;
" Thou shalt explore them, and I'll guide thee back ;
" I'll show thee many a rock, and cave, and glen,
" Where oft I've foil'd the fierce pursuit of men ;
" Teach me to be by love and thee subdu'd,
" Then blest shall be our days of solitude;
" My soul to thine shall be for ever true,
" And rolling years shall but our bliss renew;

---

[a] The fountain here alluded to is called the Waculla, and is described by Latrobe as arising in an extraordinary basin, the waters of which are formed by many subterranean springs. It had, with the aborigines, a superstitious legend connected with it, under the name of the " Fountain of Youth."    In the tale of the Natchez, it is said, " the water of this fountain can strengthen limbs bent under the weight of years, and re-embrown the hoary head of age. Eternal Spring dwells around it."    The Waculla is situate in the Floridas.

" For time shall ne'er behold our love decay—
" Age shall but ripen it from day to day;
" Speak but thy thought; whate'er it be, 'tis mine;
" My heart but throbs in unison with thine;
" And, oh! to yield thee joy were such sweet task,
" Thou need'st but only look thy wish, not ask;
" To praise the Spirit, or thy God, shall rise
" Our mingling voices to the starry skies!"
    All night she lay in sweet, unruffled sleep;
While, mindful of the charge he had to keep,
Tekarrah pac'd, observant, strict and true,
Around her bower, nor distant from his view:
Yet oft, with cautious step, he nearer drew,
Bent o'er her graceful form with raptur'd eye,
Assur'd no danger then impended nigh;
His thoughts expanded o'er a widening range,
And oft he marvell'd at the present change;
But, over all, he fondly trusted still
The Great Good Spirit would his hopes fulfil;
That He, the now sole witness of his love,
Would, from His azure fields, with smiles approve.

    Now morning's blushes mantle o'er the skies,
And early zephyrs breathe like Beauty's sighs;
The sunward clouds their draperies unfold
Of brilliant purple, edg'd with burnish'd gold;
The rhododendron, of a rose-bright hue,
Charm'd by its contrast with the waters blue;

The notes of tuneful thrush and meadow-lark
Are heard in concert with the squirrel's bark.
But ere the maiden from her slumbers wake,
'Tis fit for her he some repast should make.
Oh! love, suggestive love! with promptness glows,
If one spring fail, another fountain flows.
His ready bow and well-aim'd arrow fleet
Brought down abundant wild-fowl at his feet;
Next to prepare it he at once applied,
For want like this accustom'd to provide;
From fragments of dry wood he stripp'd the bark,
Together rubb'd them, and produc'd a spark,
Which, dropping on some sun-scorch'd leaves, became,
Fann'd by his breath, the ready wish'd-for flame;
The fire, thus kindled, hiccory branches fed,
And on the sward a savoury meal was spread.


Menana now, to greet the day, arose,
Blushing and beauteous, from her calm repose;
Beside her rustic couch, on bended knee,
She breath'd thanksgivings to the Deity;
A placid beam was playing on her face,
And lovely was she in each maiden grace.
She then approach'd Tekarrah with a smile,
Who on his task was now intent the while;
Finish'd, he led her by the hand to share
The needful succour of his woodland fare;

Their ample board was nature's verdant mould,
Their drink the calabash suffic'd to hold.

Ended their light repast; again their boat
Was on its proper element afloat;
Menana ey'd the landscape's varied range,
And felt emotions ever new and strange;
By distance sever'd from all former ties,
The once dear centre of her sympathies.
Could they so soon be dead? or could she be
Already lost to past reality;
Ah! would the shadowy future make amends
For loss of long-endear'd and faithful friends.
Such thoughts as these would on her mind intrude;
The more she shunn'd them, they the more pursu'd;
Yet could she with an unkind look repay
Her ardent lover—now her only stay?
No! but if he her heart had read, oh! there
His hope had been converted to despair.

The flowers breath'd odours, and the birds their songs
Of happiness in gay and fluttering throngs.
But though serenity around them reign'd,
Menana's bosom uncompos'd remain'd;
The passing scenes like airy fictions seem'd,
Or visions in perturbed slumbers dream'd,
Wild phantasies by reason unconfin'd,
Strange reveries—romances of the mind.

Thus, in his gallant vessel o'er the main,
The merchant, lur'd by promises of gain,
For one last venture leaves his native shore,
Haply to founder and return no more.

Menana well her heart's sad trials knew,
And knew they must be borne in silence too;
The wounded mind can know no other cure
Than resignation—firmness to endure :
Tears gush'd into her eyes, as rain-drops caught
Within the shell in time to pearls are wrought;
So might those gentle tears thereafter be
Like gems upon the brow of memory.

Still on its course their slender shallop goes,
Bearing its freight the further from their foes.
Heaven speed their way! for other help were vain,
If wanting that, though every nerve they strain.
Yet, not without a sigh, they quit once more
A transient home, a lone, but friendly shore,
Whose scents were breath'd from flowers of every dye,
And birds pour'd mellow music from the sky.
Long, long they might have tarried, unpursu'd,
In those blest haunts of peaceful solitude.
Fair was the breeze, and actively they sped
Their little bark upon its liquid bed.

Far had they steer'd, before the noon-tide blaze
Had scorch'd the woods around with fiery rays;

Then, till declining day the heat allay'd,
They sought a bank beneath a willowy shade;
But floating verdure hinder'd now their way,
And reeds and rushes thick embedded lay;
While flowers of water-plants, both white and blue,
Around them in exuberant clusters grew.
Yet they contrived, though slowly, to advance,
New objects courting still their curious glance,
Nor heeded how the moments wore along,
So happy were they those rich scenes among.
Darting from bough to bough, with sudden gleam,
The gay King-fisher skimm'd along the stream;
And 'neath the lucid wave they might behold,
*Here* soft, green moss—*there* glittering sands of gold[a].
Tekarrah felt, in each delightful pause,
An influence, such as sweetest music draws
From hallow'd feelings, recollections fond,
When to its tones they secretly respond;
For, as he clear'd away each tangling weed,
Why should he labour to increase his speed?
Was not his all, Menana, at his side?
Nor idle she, who with the paddles tried,
Dext'rous, th' opposing oziers to divide.
As thus employ'd, through labyrinths to trace,
In stooping, oft they touch'd each other's face;

---

[a] Mention is made by Du Pratz of travellers having in these parts observed grains of gold.—*History of Louisiana.*

Their breaths commingling seem'd almost as one:
Could he then wish such bliss as this to shun?
Around her waist his arm he dar'd entwine,
And whisper'd, "Oh, Menana! love, be mine!"

"Hold!" she exclaim'd, "from a long dream
    awake!
"Whate'er thou deem'st I am, thou dost mistake:
"I am not of thy race, nor of thy clime:
"My native land is far remote, and time
"Hath nearly worn its memory away;
"For dim it seems as twilight's fading ray.
"But I remember, when I was a child,
"Being days and weeks upon the waters wild.
"Vast foaming billows o'er our huge canoe
"Like mountains rose, and shut the heavens from view.
"Oh! 'twas a dreadful sight! the horrid roar!
"The winds and waves that sever'd shore from shore!
"The cries and screams that mingled with the blast,
"And every moment seeming as our last!
"Young as I was, I never can forget
"The direful scene, and tremble at it yet.
"All whom we love, how soon the deep can hide,
"As pebbles children cast upon the tide!
"While in my dear, fond mother's arms I lay,
"Above us dash'd the furious ocean's spray.
"From midnight skies, the lightning's awful flash
"Oft smote the ship before the thunder-crash;

" And one by one the crew exhausted fell,

" Amidst the mighty gulf's tempestuous swell.

" What then I felt, when came at length a wave

" That swept so many into one deep grave!

" The rest was blank! till faces wild and strange,

" And tongues unknown, gave tokens of a change;

" But what I knew not, that had o'er me come,

" For speech was useless—since its sense was dumb.

" Nor I from them, nor they from me could learn

" More than we might by sight alone discern.

" At length I thought me of the raging flood,

" And horrors then but partly understood,

" And on my mother call'd—ah! not in vain;

" Soon I was in her fond embrace again.

" Then first I saw that venerated man,

" Thy foe, my foster-father, Simaghan.

" He woo'd my mother, and her heart he won,

" And she consented to their union.

" She blest him with a pledge of mutual love,

" In whom the eagle mingled with the dove—

" A son; to me a brother; but, alas!

" Sad was our destiny: it came to pass,

" When three short summers had their blossoms shed

" Upon that dear and lovely infant's head,

" The boy, the cherish'd boy, was missing, lost,

" And all our hopes of happiness were cross'd!

" Not more than eight young springs I then had known,

" But I in early grief had elder grown.

" I wept to see my mother droop—to know
" She but indulg'd in unavailing woe.
" Her darling boy seem'd ever in her sight,
" In thoughts by day, in restless dreams by night.
" How oft in wandering fancy would she trace
" Her little lost one's innocence and grace;
" And every infant's playful voice she heard,
" Some latent feeling in her bosom stirr'd.
" Whene'er she saw a mother fondly bless'd,
" It but the more her own sad heart distress'd.
" Incessant anguish soon impair'd her brain,
" And reason fled the seat of endless pain.
" Yet it would still at times its reign resume,
" As lightning flashes through thick, starless gloom;
" But only soon again to be o'ercast—
" Such intervals were far too sweet to last.
" The Sachem strove, with all his fondest care,
" To soothe my mother in her deep despair.
" When fever rag'd and robb'd her nights of rest,
" Her burning brow with dewy moss he press'd;
" Or in the limpid stream would haste to dip
" The gourd, and bear it to her thirsty lip;
" Or gather from the near translucent pool
" The water-melon, grateful, fresh, and cool.
" We saw her health, with anguish, daily fail,
" And all our care and skill of no avail!
" She died! but with her latest breath imprest
" On me a faith thou hast not heard confest.

" As yet the Christian's Creed thou knowest not,
" Nor HIM who bled, repented sins to blot;
" And by this Sacred Cross, Eternal Sign!
" I've sworn not to forsake that faith divine,
" Nor e'er betroth myself to one of thine !
" That solemn oath I may not, dare not break,
" Not e'en, I own my fondness, for thy sake.
" I, on this relic, register my vow—
" On this reflect as time will best allow.
" But though I may not from my creed depart,
" To bear misfortune purifies the heart.
" Time may the awful barrier remove,
" And we may yet be blest in hallow'd love.
" Become a Christian! put in Heaven thy trust!
" Omnipotence is holy, wise, and just;
" And that Great Power may yet disperse thy night
" Of darkness, by His pure celestial light.
" Heaven views with equal pity every race :
" Behold yon cloud! in that an emblem trace
" Of man's regeneration from all sin;
" How black without, but, oh! how bright within !"

Her eyes betray'd the softest tenderness,
But which her tongue was tardy to confess.
While in her breast Religion's dictates strove,
Her heart was still subdu'd by mighty Love.
Though pious duty sought to break his chain,
Passion resum'd the mastery again.

And while she veil'd her face, as if in pray'r,
Tekarrah spoke in accents of despair :

" Ne'er to betroth with one of faith like mine !
" Unsay those words ! they cannot, love, be thine !
" What should I be, wert thou, indeed, untrue?
" Like a frail, lonely, drifting, lost canoe.
" Ne'er to betroth !"   " Oh ! do not look so stern,"
Exclaim'd the maid, " nor from me frowning turn !"

Those harrowing words Tekarrah mutter'd o'er,
Sucle poor Menana, faint, could say no more.
Arjbtful, he turn'd, as with a wish to see
If she suspected his fidelity ;
But to his glance her own at once replied,
Her heart, her soul did in his truth confide.

" Recall," he said, " that agonizing vow,
" Then mould me to thy will, no matter how ;
" I'll be obedient to thy slightest nod,
" And learn to worship e'en the Christian's God !"

Menana caught the words with sweet surprise,
And rais'd with joyful thanks to Heav'n her eyes ;
But half suspended yet her full delight—
Could she have heard those welcome sounds aright?
And would he swerve not from his quick resolve?
These startling questions did she now revolve,

With deep emotions, in her inmost soul;
But they surpass'd her judgment and control.
At length she breath'd, with no false blush of shame
A fervent blessing on Tekarrah's name;
Then, with a lowly, timid, downcast look,
While all her frame a sudden tremor shook,
Conscious she could not now her words recall,
She on his arm her languid head let fall,
And shed such tears as are not shed in grief,
But which came timely to the heart's relief.

Tekarrah now beheld the grateful maid
In all her loveliest, tenderest charms array'd.
The day's too sultry brightness had declin'd,
And evening with it brought a gentle wind.
Again he onward urg'd his light canoe,
Until the silvery moon shone forth anew;
And one by one the stars began to glow,
Reflected in the placid stream below.
And now he sought his little bark to moor,
And find a resting place upon the shore;
But poor Menana had already clos'd,
Unconsciously, her eye-lids, and repos'd.
Tekarrah o'er her form her mantle spread,
Then gaz'd on worlds sublime above his head;
Then dipp'd his paddles in the silent wave,
Startling the rock-bird in her mossy cave.
At length the morning broke, and with its breeze,

The fresh and fragrant hours they gladly seize,
Once more to speed them on their lingering way,
Before the sun should reach meridian day.
But soon eclips'd will be their friendly star,
By gathering clouds that menace from afar.
Hark! from the reeds the red Flamingo's cry,
Which e'er precedes the terrors of the sky;
Bright glares the East, and distant flights of Cranes
Crowd from the North, the harbingers of rains;
Along the boughs of ever-verdant oak
Ran the Savannah-rat that gusts bespoke[a].
Such signs, too sure, foretel a coming storm,
And dangers brooding, in their direst form.
Menana view'd, alarm'd, each threatening cloud,
The waves were ruffled, and the winds blew loud;
Their frail and feeble skiff was rudely tost,
And oft she dreaded would be wholly lost;
No sheltering bay, no haven safe was near,
The haze grew thicker, and the scene more drear,
And now the clouds their deluge downward send,
And lightnings seem the earth and heaven to rend.
The Spirit of the Tempest vents his wrath—
But, hold! what light illumes them on their path?
Perchance some recent embers, left as dead,
Have partially revivified and spread

---

[a] Chateaubriand.

To sun-dried leaves and res'nous boughs of trees,
The flame of which expands before the breeze.
Whate'er the cause, Menana shrunk with fear,
And thoughts of absent friends and wigwams dear.
But still she struggled to conceal alarm,
Not to unnerve her toiling lover's arm;
While he, encourag'd by the look she gave,
Still urg'd his boat upon the heaving wave.


Hours had elaps'd, the storm abated not,
And now she half bemoan'd her hapless lot;
Loud thunder-peals, like earthquakes of the sky,
Appear'd to shake the firmament on high,
Struck by the lightning's shaft, whole forests blaze;
Appall'd, upon the awful scene they gaze.
Borne by the winds aloft, the meteor-flakes
Destruction spread, or fall in hissing lakes;
Time-honor'd trees are thickly strewn around,
And all their branches levell'd with the ground;
The sturdiest monarchs of the leafy realm,
Ages had fail'd to bow, or storms to whelm,
Now yielded to the tempest's furious sway,
That swept at once their pride and strength away.
The Crane and Cormorant, 'midst flame and smoke,
Expire beneath the elemental stroke.
A fatal horror ushers in the night,
While howling beasts increase the wild affright.

Ill-fated pair! their strength was nearly spent,
When calmer grew the troubled firmament;
But marvel 'twas to see their little bark
Still safe upon the waters, like the Ark
That held the remnant of a world destroy'd,
To fill again the universal void.
But hark! what sound excites the startled maid?
It is delusion! why that look dismay'd?
Tekarrah heard it not, but with surprise
Beheld Menana's eager, anxious eyes,
As loud she shriek'd, " My mother's voice I hear!"
And wildly gaz'd with mingled hope and fear.
Tekarrah listen'd; but he heard no more
Than the lone, sullen splashing of his oar.
No wonder if he for a moment thought
Some potent spell upon her mind had wrought;
Yet, no! though seem'd her memory in a trance,
She still shew'd reason in her stedfast glance;
And now he heard himself a vocal strain,
By distance mellow'd o'er the liquid plain.
But she still fancied, in that lonely scene,
It only could her mother's voice have been,
The tones of which, upon her ravish'd ear,
Seem'd as if wafted from a heavenly sphere:
And as the last notes softly died away,
She knew it was her mother's sacred lay;
That Vesper-hymn Menana had been taught
By her who first had train'd her infant thought.

But who could chaunt that solemn anthem here,
Where all was savage, desolate, and drear?

Imagination oft fantastic sees
Things not in being—images in trees.
Thus may distemper'd minds the reason shake,
And shadowy shapes for living forms mistake;
Oft too the ear may be deceiv'd awhile,
And fancied strains the listener's soul beguile.

As on they veer'd, a faint and glimmering light
Upon the foreland met their anxious sight,
And near the top a wattled dwelling stood,
Not far from which was rais'd a cross of wood;
A symbol sacred to Menana's sight,
And filling all her soul with pure delight;
For could she doubt that hut was the abode
Of some lone Christian-worshipper of God?
A human figure, moving to and fro,
Seem'd to invite them to a creek below;
A lighted torch he bore, wherewith to aid
Strangers, if any such had thither stray'd.
'Twas he Menana's mother deem'd as dead,
But who had from the wreck escap'd and fled;
That spot for years had been his dwelling place,
A holy man of distant clime and race;
There he in age and piety had grown,
And only to the scatter'd natives known;

His drink the rill, his food the juicy plant,
The moss his bed, the wood his lonely haunt.
Few sins he had his conscience to oppress,
Peace his companion, Heaven his happiness.

The stranger lent the pair his willing aid,
And up a rough-hewn pathway led the maid,
To chambers scoop'd from out the solid rock,
That frown'd defiance at the tempest's shock.
Tekarrah made his trustful bark secure,
Then trac'd his steps instinctively and sure.
The wanderers found within the hermit's cave
No plenteous store—but what he had, he gave.
His pine-torch soon reviv'd a cheerful flame,
Whose warmth was welcome to Menana's frame;
Meanwhile the friendly, hospitable sage,
With all the busy nimbleness of age,
Spread on the rugged trunk of some huge tree
Coarse bread and honeycomb of woodland-bee;
In cups of cane-reed knot, cut near the root,
He pour'd bright beverage of the vinous fruit;
And when he bade his guests partake his fare,
Menana touch'd it not, until in pray'r
She had her solemn, silent thanks exprest,
And kiss'd the cross upon the pilgrim's breast.
The goodly man, with sudden awe amaz'd,
With looks benignant on the maiden gaz'd,
Inquisitive to read her inmost thought,
As if she'd been miraculously taught;

Or else how could that heathen-born adore
The sacred sign he on his tunic wore.
She now became still dearer to his breast,
By the religion she had thus confest.
Tekarrah, too, was not without a share
In the good man's solicitude and care.
Menana long in secrecy had sigh'd
To find some reverend, pious, Christian guide;
But until now her hopes had been denied.
Of men of holy mission she had heard,
And pin'd to listen to the Godly Word,
Such men, she knew, had rang'd the wild, the wood,
To wean the Indian from a thirst of blood;
Her mother's shade she deem'd would bless the hour
That saw her under such protecting power.
Hence had her mind, though wav'ring from the first,
Striv'n to repress the flame Tekarrah nurs'd;
Though to his vows a willing ear she lent,
Oft she in secret would the act repent.
One strong desire alone the maid controll'd,
One only hope supported and consol'd;
The sole fond object of her thought by day,
Her dreams by night as on her couch she lay,
Was how to sway Tekarrah to the truth,
And lead to heaven the unconverted youth.
What rapture then her throbbing bosom felt,
As now she oft in Christian worship knelt
With the good father, while Tekarrah mus'd,
Nor yet assented, nor assent refus'd;

Her only aim to draw the wav'ring chief
Within the circle of her own belief;
For, as his mind was partly now imprest,
She wisely judg'd that time would work the rest.

END OF CANTO THE FIFTH.

# MENANA.

---

## CANTO VI.

---

"Grief is but guess'd when thou art standing by:
But I too soon shall know what absence is;
Why, 'tis to be no more; another name for death."

OLD PLAY.

---

AMIDST the loveliest scenery of hills,
Of plains and valleys, and meandering rills,
Where scarlet flowering maple-buds appear,
When Spring renews the freshness of the year;
And the lone ever-sombre cypress grows,
Emblems of Youth's bright blush and tender woes;
Where tremulously shake the aspen's leaves,
And the wake-robin plant its texture weaves;

While closely ambush'd in its perfum'd bow'r,
The wild bee sips the Dionœa flow'r;
Here stood Menana's hut, between two groves,
In which the dappled deer pursu'd their loves,
A shaded arbour in a sultry land,
With sun or shelter ever at command;
Near it a spring, with flowers about the brink,
Whose limpid water woo'd the lip to drink;
Around an ample tree a circled space
Was trimly clear'd, to be her dwelling place.
There stakes were closely set, and knit between
With pliant twigs, to form a porchway green,
Whose trellis'd summit left the cluster'd vine
Above its ringlets freely to entwine.
With cordage from the Anotta-tree supplied
The wicker outwork dexterously was tied;
Within 'twas furnish'd with a simple seat,
And the light proa, firmly built and fleet;
Her grass-net hammock, high and pendant hung,
From sturdy cedar boughs securely slung;
The rustic roof with reeds and leaves o'erspread,
And wreath'd with flow'rs, thus form'd her humble shed;
And soon beneath the builder's hand it sprung[a],
His will was eager, and his strength was young.

---

[a] "In a few hours they finish a hut, the bark-roof of which frequently covers more happiness than the domes of palaces."— *Chateaubriand's Travels*, vol. i, p. 203.

There from the morning's dawn till eventide,
That chosen spot their utmost wants supplied;
From their own hearts their sole delights they drew,
What one enamour'd, charm'd the other too.
Thus bliss serene oft seeks the shady dell,
And shuns the heights where pride and envy dwell.
Love builds his nest amidst secluded bowers,
Far more securely than in lofty towers.
There, where the humming-bird on blooming spray
Flew to avoid the burning glare of day,
Seeking the chalice of some lovely rose,
In whose sweet leaves the dewy nectar flows;
There, where the foliage soften'd summer's beam,
Love wove the texture of his magic dream.
If languid, in the fervid heat of day,
Reposing in her sleeping-net she lay,
Outside her hut Tekarrah vigil kept,
To guard her from intrusion while she slept;
Or oft they sat in some cool arbour's shade,
While feathery songsters grateful music made;
Or, when it seem'd as if the orb of night
Look'd down upon them with serene delight,
She was the shrine at which his fondest sighs
Were offer'd as love's votive sacrifice.
O'er these broad scenes, array'd in sober hues,
Her soul with tranquil nature lov'd to muse;
Lov'd to behold fair isles in clusters glide,
Trembling and twinkling down the rippling tide,

Where 'gainst the margin of each green retreat
The gentle wavelets of the current beat,
And where the light-stirr'd tinted foliage play'd
With the soft shadows which the moonbeams made,
And there she felt how sweet was solitude,
Compar'd with men and manners wild and rude.
Why should the wretched seek some savage den,
Rather than harbour 'midst the haunts of men,
But that they covet little, save repose,
And dread in men alone their deadliest foes?

Within the woods, Tekarrah and the maid,
Near the good Monk, beheld a summer fade,
By him and his persuasion there delay'd.
The Chief, whose hut was near Menana's rear'd,
Ever to do her least behest appear'd;
He read her lightest wishes in her look,
And to anticipate them pleasure took.
Maize-flow'rs and silken willow-buds were spread,
With down of cotton-rush to rest her head;
These for her pillow were each morning brought,
By him who e'en her smallest comfort sought.
Her task meanwhile was to attend each flow'r
That wildly grew about her rustic bow'r.
The hymn, too, learn'd in infancy, she sung,
And through the woods the notes melodious rung;
While on some neighbouring pine the mocking-bird
Listen'd to imitate the sounds he heard;

F

Then flew from branch to branch, and tree to tree,
To echo back her vocal harmony.
The feather'd choir seem'd pleas'd to linger near,
And at her voice approach'd, devoid of fear;
The gentle robin careless hopp'd around,
And peck'd the crumbs she strew'd upon the ground;
That fleet, wild commoner, the timorous hare[a],
Play'd on the greensward, unmolested there.
Like them she learn'd all terror to discard,
Secure in innocence, that heavenly guard.
Apart the Hermit in his rocky cell,
As long had been his wont, preferr'd to dwell;
In pray'rs and penitence his hours were spent,
Though little had that good man to repent.
But oft he left the calm, secluded place,
To train his children in the paths of grace;
Who fondly liv'd, congenial in each thing,
Like the twin colours on th' halcyon's wing.
No more she strove her feelings to subdue,
Which partially repress'd, the stronger grew.
He like the sun to her did joy impart;
She was to him the rainbow of the heart.

---

[a] Imlay, on America, has affirmed that there was not a wild
hare in the whole of that continent. This is a gross error. The
Indian name for the American hare is Warpoos, and is, I believe,
the *Lepus Americanus* of Linnæus. Martyn, in his Elements of
Natural History, describes the difference of form in the North
American hare. There is one in the British Museum.

Thus did they daily dwell in love; yet still
Their passion made obedient to the will.


Kind Nature minister'd to every need,
For Nature there was bountiful indeed.
Wild though the spot, it yielded truest wealth,
Calm joys, sound sleep, light labour, strength, and
    health.


Still on the past Menana's thoughts would turn;
For who would not for absent lov'd ones yearn?
Still she recall'd in memory's wild romance
Her young companions in the lightsome dance,
When carelessly she mingled in the throng,
To the rude music, and the ruder song.
With these some hallow'd griefs, perhaps, might blend;
But hope soon chas'd them, an unfailing friend.
Yet she would fain once more have gaz'd around
On the rich prairies where she lov'd to bound;
Where she had form'd her simple, rude recess,
A leafy alcove in the wilderness.
It was an Eden thus created there
For unforbidden joys; and birds of rare
And gaudy plumage glitter'd in the air.
Nor marvel if at times her gentle heart
Would heave a sigh, or bid the tear-drop start;

But ever was Tekarrah at her side,
Softly to soothe, or tenderly to chide.
Though here were scented groves and golden skies,
Less lovely were they in Menana's eyes,
Less beautiful, though gorgeous all appear'd,
Than distant scenes to memory endear'd;
A lovely moss-bank, or a murmuring stream,
Where she had once indulg'd young Fancy's dream,
Far more she priz'd than Nature's grander views,
In all their blended charms and varied hues.


Yet think not always sadden'd was her look:
No; oft it seem'd as placid as the brook
O'er which the moon-beams throw their modest light,
Upon a summer's clear and cloudless night.
And when she pastime sought in idle hours,
She gather'd store of herbs, and plants, and flow'rs,
Extracting from them all their healing pow'rs.
Nor was she from domestic duties free;
These she discharg'd as 'twere instinctively.
Reason had taught her, too, with grace to bend,
To learn the useful, and the faulty mend.
But more than this, the Book of sacred lore,
Which from the wreck the pious hermit bore,
She daily lov'd to pause and ponder o'er;
Till from its pages, with enraptur'd eyes,
She caught a glimpse of bliss beyond the skies.

One morn, equipp'd to chase, with ample scope,
For savoury food, the flying antelope,
Tekarrah came to bid the maid adieu
In accents tender and with fervour true.


" I grieve," he said, "to leave thee; but I go,
" Soon to return with spoils upon my bow;
" Let not my absence give thy bosom pain,
" Fleet as the winds I will return again!"


" I know not how it is," the maid replied—
And as she spoke, she half-unconscious sighed—
" But I would have thee stay; for ne'er till now
" Felt I such anxious throbbing on my brow.
" When thou hast left me for the chase before,
" Light was my heart, that nought foreboded more
" Than a few hours of solitary thought,
" Until again my pleasure back was brought.
" Thus scenes around me prov'd or dark or fair,
" As thou wert absent or wert present there.
" Our progress hither seems almost a dream;
" Our little bark upon the moonlit stream,
" The rippling sound it waken'd as it went,
" The verdant shore and spangled firmament,
" The night-bird's song, the waving water-flowers,
" All these beguil'd our many lonely hours;

" And dearer now their images remain,
" When such, alas ! we ne'er may see again !
" For, oh ! I feel as some impending ill
" Were hovering o'er us, and my blood runs chill !
" What shall console me while thou art away ?
" But if thy loving thoughts shall with me stay,
" Hope may sustain me till thy wish'd return,
" And then I'll cease to doubt and cease to mourn."


" Be not alarm'd, my own belov'd," he said ;
" Dry up those tears, although for me they're shed ;
" This greenwood shelter shall, sweet maiden, be
" The safe abode of pure tranquillity ;
" Ere long our warm affection shall entwine,
" As loving tendrils wreath around the vine.
" Would'st thou away with *me ?*   Ah ! say not so !
" I leave thee safer here, and singly go ;
" Too sensitive, Menana, is thy heart ;
" The rustling of a leaf would make thee start ;
" The tremulous hind is not of gentler mood
" Than thou, by thy timidity subdu'd ;
" With forest dangers thou could'st ill contend ;
" In the dread storm thy fragile form would bend ;
" Our wilder scenes thy nature ill would suit ;
" A breeze may shake to earth the fairest fruit.
" Thou know'st my prowess, fleetness, strength of arm ;
" These will protect me, sweet, from every harm !

" The charm'd drop-feather,[a] too, thou see'st I wear,
" And that alone, love, should dispel thy care."

" Well, Heaven be with thee! but till thou return,
" My heart will languish, and my brow will burn;
" And should some dire mischance thy steps detain,
" Or should I ne'er behold thy face again,
" Yet, although absent, I will think thee near,
" And fancy, in the lake, broad, bright and clear,
" I see thy shadow walking at my side,
" As thou wert wont at lonely eventide;
" Still view thine image, by the moonlight rays
" Reflected, like my own desponding gaze;
" Or should I chance to meet some antler'd hind,
" The noble animal will bring to mind
" How oft thou hast in triumph from the chase
" Return'd, to clasp me in thy dear embrace.
" When I behold in nests, securely hung,
" The parent birds protect their unfledg'd young,
" Or teach them by degrees to cleave the sky,
" They will remind me of thine infancy.
" Whate'er in nature seems replete with truth
" Will but recall the image of thy youth;
" When thou art present, nothing more I need;
" When absent, love shall on thy memory feed;

---

[a] The drop-feather of an eagle's wing renders the wearer invincible and invulnerable, and the Indians generally consider the feathers of the eagle possessed of occult and sovereign virtues.—*Tour on the Prairies.*

" And when I close my weary eyes at night,
" Thy visionary form shall glad my sight."

 " Calm all thy thoughts till I return," he said ;
" Fancy no danger, and be not afraid ;
" No lurking pitfalls will my steps betray,
" Thy love is with me, and 'tis open day ;
" The valleys bask in sunbeams and in bloom,
" Thou only, dearest, wear'st a face of gloom ;
" And for the sighs thou breathest for my sake,
" I could half chide thee, lest thy heart should break ;
" But to the ' Great Good Spirit's man'ᵃ we'll walk,
" And he shall soothe thee with his Wisdom-talk."ᵇ

 Thus from her mind he tried to wean a care
He deem'd that reason should not harbour there ;
Then left her at the Hermit's rocky cell,
After a loving gaze and fond farewell,
Bounding with speed upon his usual track.
But long his absence, and he came not back.
Menana felt a thousand fears in one,
As though her troubles had but now begun.
When night-clouds sail'd along the azure sky,
Where all was beauty and serenity,
Then in her bosom agonizing throbs
Were to the moon confess'd, in tears and sobs.

---

ᵃ The Priest.     ᵇ The Bible.

She then recall'd his parting tenderness,
And wherefore leave her in such deep distress?
Could he be faithless?   Oh! that dreadful thought,
Was with unutterable anguish fraught!
Confus'd, bewilder'd, still she would repeat
His parting words, for parting words are sweet.

END OF CANTO THE SIXTH.

# MENANA.

## CANTO VII.

DAY followed day, but still came not the chief,
And from the monk the maiden sought relief;
But he could scarce his own deep grief assuage,
To him each lingering hour appear'd an age.
He trusted to have joined in holy bands—
Their hearts already one—their willing hands,
And thus to sanctify their earthly love
By that pure union register'd above.
The noon-tide sun diffus'd its flood of light
In one broad blaze, unutterably bright;
Still had Menana—since the earliest dawn
Had tipp'd the mountain-top or streak'd the lawn,

Despite the luminary's dazzling rays—
Intently fix'd her anxious, eager gaze,
Expectant, hoping, as she watch'd his track,
Once more to'see him, joyous, bounding back.
And still she look'd, and wept, and watch'd in vain;
But he came not to mitigate her pain.
Another and another day there came,
And each to her sad drooping soul the same.
Oft she would from a silent reverie start,
As though a sudden pang had pierc'd her heart;
Now to her frenzied eye his form appears,
In every view suggested by her fears;
Now she beholds him by his foes waylaid,
Or in some ambush suddenly betray'd.
Some other turn her wandering mind pursu'd,
But still one object haunted every mood.
Delirious fancy chang'd her hour by hour,
As wayward sense might reason overpow'r,
While tears, with which her eyes were ever fraught,
Roll'd down her cheeks as fugitive as thought.


And sometimes, when the good old pilgrim slept,
She from his guardian care in silence crept;
Then through the wood, the thicket, glen, or glade,
Seeking for something lost, alone she stray'd;
Where serpents, perhaps, lay coil'd in seeming sleep,
Or through the groves where generous maples weep

For thirsty travellers refreshing drink [a],
Sweeter than from the fountain's cooling brink.
Heaven only mark'd her footsteps and distress,
As thus she linger'd in her wretchedness;
But, in her search, where'er she roam'd, 'twas vain,
And, unconsol'd, she wander'd back again.


One day she rambled to the higher land,
That she might greater space of view command;
And there, while gazing from the lofty height,
A numerous armament soon met her sight.
Near and more near, in many a long canoe,
A formidable host of warriors drew;
And by full many an unforgotten sign
Their hateful purpose she could well divine.
In eager haste they sought a neighbouring bay,
Where the vast concourse, rang'd at random, lay;
But soon they crowded to the shore's extent,
On some great sacrifice or object bent.
Some their war-weapons scan with curious eye,
The keenness of their tomahawks they try,

---

[a] "The American maple bears no resemblance to the tree of the same name in Europe. The former yields a sap, which has a much pleasanter taste than the best lemonade. This liquor is produced by making incisions into the wood."—See *Pinkerton's Voyages*, vol. xiii, p. 539.

Both spike and edge, firmly the head secur'd,
And the haft fitly to the hand assur'd;
Their scalping knives, next, from their cloaks beneath
They draw, to test if easy in the sheath.


A venerable chief was at their head,
And in their train a captive youth was led.
Menana felt her soul prophetic grow
Of some yet undefin'd impending woe.
Her hurried gaze o'er every object ran—
She knew the tribe was that of Simaghan.
Awhile she held unconsciously her breath,
For well she deem'd some chief was doom'd to death;
Still they advanc'd, until so near they came,
That she discern'd her lover's manly frame.
It was indeed the captive lost so long,
And now the victim of a vengeful throng.
One piercing shriek to heaven she wildly sent,
Then toward the tribe her flying footsteps bent.


On that sad morning, when Tekarrah left
Menana full of fears, of joy bereft,
He, conscious not of danger lurking nigh,
Was led beyond his wonted boundary,
When suddenly and unsuspected rose,
Before, behind, about him, bands of foes:

So secretly they sprang and hemm'd him round,
That he was instantly disarm'd and bound,
Without a struggle and without a wound;
While yells of joy resounded to the skies,
For well they knew the value of their prize.
Scouts were they from the camp of Simaghan,
Who now his homeward journey had began;
Having reveng'd some injury or disgrace
Upon a nation of a hostile race.
Some coasted round the long and winding beach,
While others landward sought their point to reach;
To meet by concert at the headland, where
Menana first beheld them wending there.
Thus had Tekarrah fallen in their power,
In an unguarded and too fatal hour.

Menana's wonted fortitude return'd,
And now love only in her bosom burn'd.
She yet might save him from the fatal brand,
She yet might stay the dread, uplifted hand.
Vain thought! Menana, little dost thou know
Thou can'st not now retrieve him from the foe.
The astonish'd crowd beheld the maid advance,
Unterrified by each opposing lance.
At first she call'd upon Tekarrah's name,
And then on Simaghan's; at length she came
To where the hero bound and guarded lay,
The destin'd victim of the coming day.

Tekarrah heard the voice he lov'd so well,
But with what mingled feelings who can tell?
" And can it be?   How cam'st thou, dearest, here?
" Hast thou not wing'd thy way from yon bright
          sphere?
" Or dost thou yet to this dim earth belong,
" Already old to me, though yet so young?
" Methinks thou art the hunter's welcome star,[a]
" Whose stedfast light he views with joy afar.
" Can'st thou, my own, my sweet Menana be?
" What shall requite this proof of love for me?
" 'Tis pain to see thee thus so pale and faint,
" Woe in thy looks, but on thy tongue no plaint.
" Yet welcome is this love renew'd to me,
" Like dew to flowers, or sunshine to the bee!
" Oh! from the death scene, dearest trembler, fly!
" Nor wait the circling flame, ascending high,
" To bear my spirit to its parent sky."

" My panting heart rejoices to behold
" Thy face again!" she said; " I'm now consol'd;
" They shall not part us more, to thee I'll cling,
" 'Till from the Sachem I forgiveness wring.
" Sole object of my anxious hope and pray'r,
" Yet will I save thee! I will not despair!

---

[a] The North Star, in the beautifully poetical language of the
Red Indians, " The star which never moves," " The hunter's star."

" Ne'er shall thy blue-ey'd maid of other lands
" Resign her warrior at the foe's commands.
" Through dark or sunny scenes, still let me find
" One faithful bosom, and one gentle mind.
" We to our wild home will once more away,
" And never, never shalt thou from me stray;
" There where we oft have spent such pleasing hours,
" Screen'd from the sultry heat by leaves and flow'rs,
'· There, as we gaze on Nature's lovely zone,
" We'll dream her charms were made for us alone;
" For life with good or ill is only fraught
" As we ourselves but make it in our thought.
" Thus, poor or rich, we so esteem the mind
" As we're ourselves to good or ill inclin'd.
" We yet shall happy, happy be for years!
" Ah, no! that hope is banish'd still by fears;
" For while my lips speak what my heart dictates,
" Truth rushes in and blackens both our fates.
" How throbs my brain! I do but only dream!
" 'Tis maddening fancy—a wild, idle scheme—·
" Did'st thou not go to chase the nimble deer?
" Did'st thou not tell me thou had'st nought to fear?
" And can'st thou be again a captive bound,
" Fix'd by those cruel fastenings to the ground?
" Can we not realize again those hours,
" When we were blest like birds in leafy bow'rs?
" But, hark! that shout! I hear the horrid cry!
" They claim the sacrifice! Thou shalt not die!

" Yet, ah ! how shaftless is thy quiver now;

" How useless, too, thy once unerring bow !

" Yes ! they may tear me limb from limb, but ne'er

" Shall sever us !"

     " Menana, love, forbear !

" For now to cherish hope, alas ! were vain;

" I ne'er shall breathe in liberty again.

" Such hopes are like the Magic Isle, that woos

" The sight, but flies before our swift canoes.ᵃ

" Brief as the stroke of paddles on the lake

" Is now the life devoted for thy sake.

" Thy destiny must ne'er be link'd with mine,

" But hours of happiness may yet be thine ;

" Still like the clinging-plant to thee I'd cleave,

" Till the Great Spirit should my soul receive.

" And though I find I still am lov'd by thee,

" I feel unmann'd, and would once more be free ;

" But clearest streams will sometimes turbid grow,

" There is not always purity in snow.

" Nature herself can things unequal make ;

" A gloomy cave beside a lovely lake.

---

ᵃ The Indians of Florida relate, says Chateaubriand, that in the centre of a lake there is an island, where dwell the most beautiful women in the world. The Muscogulges, a neighbouring nation of the Natchez, set out several times to attempt the conquest of the magic island; but the Elysian retreat fleeing before their canoes, at length disappeared.

" But must I bid to thee and life adieu?

" A cloud is o'er me and my fate in view!

" To die—yet live within the hearts of those

" We love—cannot be death, but sweet repose."


" Oh, fatal hour!" exclaimed the weeping maid,

" To see thee thus to ruthless foes betray'd!

" Too well my shrinking heart forboded guile,

" When last I look'd upon thy parting smile,

" When last we sojourn'd in sweet solitude,

" Where all was free that was with life endu'd!

" But I will ask not what mischance befel;

" These bonds too fatally the issue tell.

" No, no; my way I'll to the Sachem cleave,

" And sue for pity and a quick reprieve!

" He lov'd me once, he was my second sire,

" And I may yet restrain his cruel ire."


" 'Tis vain! Menana, stay!" the captive said;

" I now shall soon be number'd with the dead.

" As eagles for their prey, war-chiefs for fame

" Brave every danger and pursue their aim;

" I never more shall climb the mountain-steep,

" Nor ply my paddle on the glassy deep.

" I had resolv'd, ere pass'd were two moons more,

" Thy Christian God, Menana, to adore;

" Then with my native tribe and thee to dwell:

" But now, my treasur'd love, my all, farewell!

" Thou said'st the cross in mercy was design'd
" To be a blissful token to mankind ;
·" To teach us here with patience to endure,
" And point the path that leads to regions pure.
" To me it has not prov'd that happy sign,
" Nor have I marked its influence divine ;
" For where that symbol floated in the air,
" War, blood, and death were sure to follow there.
" May it not be, the Spirit Great and Good—
" In awe of whom my reverent fathers stood—
" Whom, for thy Saviour's sake, I would have left,
" Has now my fickle heart of hope bereft ?"

Menana shudder'd, as with solemn brow
She caught his words, then answer'd calm and low :
" That thought, Tekarrah, from thy soul dismiss,
" As we would meet again in realms of bliss ;
" I fondly hop'd that in thy breast had grown
" The same belief I feel within my own.
" Though far from friends, from home, from country
      driv'n,
" One hope remains, one sure resource—in heav'n !"
Clasping her hands, she, darting through the throng,
Sought Simaghan the elder chiefs among.

Tekarrah's guards beheld the scene, surpris'd ;
But well they knew Menana, though disguis'd,
Disguis'd by deep and overwhelming grief,
The long-reputed daughter of their chief,

And perhaps they yet some latent feeling bore
Of kindness too, to one so lov'd before.

Soon she appear'd within the Sachem's view,
And thus began for lenity to sue:
" Dear father! mighty Sachem! honor'd sire!
" Suspend thy vengeance, oh! avert thine ire;
" Teach by example to be just and wise,
" And spare for once this menac'd sacrifice.
" White men show mercy, Red Men should forgive,
" Soften your wrath, and let your captive live;
" Lest the GREAT SPIRIT should indignant rouse,
" And smite ye by the terrors of his brows.
" Respect your foe; for in his native land
" He still hath friends and warriors[a] at command,
" Thick as the birds protected from the breeze
" Within the hanging moss of yonder trees;
" And clouds of arrows from their bows may fly,
" If thou condemn their youthful chief to die.
" By all that's generous, merciful and brave,
" Let me implore his pardon! save him! save!"

Exhausted, now she sunk upon the ground,
But soon was rais'd by those who stood around.

---

[a] The Natchez have always been represented as a numerous and powerful race, as may be seen in Du Pratz; and, according to Latrobe, they were always considered a superior tribe of the Red Indians.

The Sachem frown'd, but some emotion came
To thrill his breast and agitate his frame;
At length he sternly answer'd her appeal,
Although he might some secret pity feel.

" His darts may cloud the air like flakes of snow!
" But, foolish maid, a warrior loves his foe
" As the fierce Catamount[a] the tender doe.
" Deceitful words, how smooth so e'er they seem,
" Are like a bright, but poison-tainted stream.
" Thou hast the sleeky beaver's subtlety,
" That climbs for what it loves the slender tree,
" To feed upon the buds with juices rife,
" And rob the young branch of its leaves of life.[b]
" Thou'rt like infected garments white men wear,
" That bring the plague-spot[c] and pollute the air;
" A stranger to our climate and our race,
" Blanch'd is thy skin, and smooth thine artful face;

---

[a] The Catamount is a kind of wild cat, as high as the tiger, but thinner, and his skin is extremely beautiful; fortunately his species is now rare.—*History of Louisiana*, p. 263.

[b] It is well known that the beaver will at the risk of its life climb the tallest poplars of the forest, for the juicy leaves of those trees. In like manner, it has been said that this animal will climb a slender tree, the leaves of which wither and die as soon as they are touched; to this last statement the reader may attach what credence he pleases.—See *Tales of an Indian Camp*, vol. iii, p. 50.

[c] Small Pox.

" The Red Man's bosom feels the quicken'd glow
" Of nature stronger than 'pale people' know :
" Yet I remember thee once like a dove,
" Breathing of beauty, innocence, and love ;
" Pure as the snow-fall ere the dawn has broke
" And ting'd its whiteness with the wigwam's smoke ;
" But then I dream'd not of thy serpent art,
" Coiling around my unsuspecting heart.
" Some beauteous shrubs may yield us wholesome fruit,
" Yet bear a deadly poison at the root.[a]
" 'Tis well thou dost remind me of the time
" That link'd my fondness with deceitful crime.
" Did I not snatch thee from the 'Great Salt Lake,'
" And bear my tribe's derision for thy sake?
" Thy raiment of a texture slight and thin
" I caus'd to be exchang'd for Marten-skin ;[b]
" Did I not deck thee with our richest beads[c]
" And rarest shells, whose beauty none exceeds?
" Did I not rear thee like a gentle doe,

---

[a] Among the few poisonous plants of Canada is a shrub which yields a wholesome fruit, but contains in its roots a deadly juice, which the widow who wishes not to survive her husband drinks.— *Notices of the Canadian Indians, by Edward Walsh, M.D.*

[b] The skin of the marten is the most delicate imaginable, and is esteemed as the greatest luxury.

[c] Some shells are beautiful, says Du Pratz, and blue ones are found much esteemed, and have long been in request for tobacco-boxes.

" Spar'd timely from the cruel Carcajou?ª

" And on thee all a father's care bestow?

" When flights of birdsᵇ flew o'er our camp, and told

" By gabbling signs the coming winter's cold;

" When howl'd the wind, or fell the heavy rain,

" Shelter'd and warm thou hast securely lain;

" From both protected was thy fragile form,

" Guarded from drifting snow and sleety storm.

" No gentle maiden of our own descent

" Had e'er so many furs within her tent.

" In summer, when was vocal every spray,

" If thou didst from my hide-bound wigwam stray,

" What ' red skin ' was not pleas'd if thou didst share

" His own kind roof and hospitable fare?

" What maiden who with us could kindred claim

" Had e'er incurr'd such voluntary shame ?

" Had any of *my* race been foster'd thus

" By '*pale-fac'd ones*,' as thou hast been by us,

" Would she have dar'd their friendship to repay

" With base ingratitude,—the white man's way?

---

ª The Carcajou, or wild cat, is the natural enemy of the elk species.—See *Charlevoix*.

ᵇ " The weather, too, had given tokens of change, and of the approach of the southern winter; and as we lay round our fires at night, we heard the whistling pinions of innumerable geese and ducks, winging their way from the north to a more genial climate. The beauty of the year had indeed passed away."—*Latrobe's Rambler in North America.*

" Or, having once against them basely striv'n,

" With crafty tears have sued to be forgiv'n?

" 'Tis this that rankles to my inmost soul,

" And rouses feelings age may not control.

" But wherefore do I idly waste my breath,

" Or thus delay the signal for his death?

" When points the shadow of yon lofty pine

" To the near brook—revenge shall then be mine:

" Then, bound and ready for the sacrifice,

" The victim 'neath the fiercest torture dies.

" By him we've lost our warriors in their pride,

" By him our wise old men of grief have died;

" What spouseless squaws cry loud for vengeance due?

" What children weep, whose sires his weapon slew?

" E'en now their unseen spirits may float by,

" Or from the land of souls our woes descry.

" My burning rage no longer shall be pent,

" But fire-words from my lips shall find a vent!

" Our greatest foe is once more in our thrall,

" And with one blow the topmost tree shall fall;

" His blood is not more precious in his veins

" Than that which flows in ours; the deep red stains

" Left by his hand upon our slaughter'd race,

" His own heart's current only can efface;

" Like the marsh-meteor's false and fleeting ray,

" His light shall pass in lurid clouds away.

" For thee, who cut the bond-cord of my foe,

" No more my wigwam's shelter shalt thou know;

" Hence ! perish with the idol of thy heart,
" Or first behold his death-pangs and depart !
" Expect no pity from the red-man's breast,
" Thou hast thyself to answer for the rest ;
" Think not he shall again escape his doom,
" Soon shall the flames his quivering limbs consume ;
" But I will grant thee more than thy desire,
" For thou shalt see him in those flames expire ;
" His dying tortures will the keener be,
" That thou art witness of his agony ;
" And 'twill our vengeance but the more refine,
" To know his pangs will only add to thine ! "


" Oh, Sachem ! spurn me not ! " the maiden cried,
" Nor my entreaties cruelly deride !
" Has age the current of thy blood congeal'd ?
" Will not thy heart to gentle pity yield ?
" Do youthful feelings die with youthful years ?
" Are fathers senseless to their children's tears ?
" Hoar Age should like a tender parent be
" To younger offspring of humanity.
" Good actions are like golden fruits, they blow
" Luxuriant in the Summer's brilliant glow ;
" Revenge is indiscriminate and wild,
" But age should not of mercy be beguil'd ;
" As canker-worms in ripest cores abound,
" So evil in the purest hearts is found ;

" Or as rich pearls with poorer are combin'd,

" Thoughts fair and foul are blended in the mind;

" Then do not thou afford within thy breast

" A sanctuary for a hideous guest.

" Oft hast thou fondly plac'd me on thy knee,

" Pleas'd, then, my childhood's artless wiles to see;

" Oft kiss'd my cheeks, and smooth'd my hair, and said,

" I was thy favorite—thy blue-eyed maid;

" And that my voice was like the murmuring

" Of the sweet music of the streams in spring;

" But now thou spurn'st me, Sachem! from thy sight,

" And in my anguish feel'st a keen delight;

" Oh, that I could recall thy tenderness,

" Or that I ne'er had known thy fond caress!

" Behold me prostrate at thy feet, and hear;

" Tekarrah never felt revenge or fear,

" He only sought to conquer cruel foes,

" Who spar'd not even women in their woes;

" The poor, the sick, the helpless or insane;

" Nor did he e'er thy sacred rites profane;

" The wise he honor'd, paid to age respect,

" Nor the infirm e'er treated with neglect;

" His name thou hast most wrongfully revil'd,

" And for his doom the deadly fire-frame[a] pil'd."

---

ᵃ The Indians put their prisoners of war into a kind of frame, made with two posts and a pole laid across, and burn them alive.

Too much oppress'd, she sank in grief profound,
Cold as a marble statue, on the ground;
White were her cheeks as the pure lotus bloom,
Yet no one sought to dissipate her gloom.
But though awhile subdu'd her tender form,
Her firmness waver'd not: so in the storm
The wrestler of the waves his breast upheaves,
Till, struggling, to some anchorage he cleaves.

But hark! those yells, like furious battle-shouts,
Rais'd when his foes some mighty warrior routs;
Fierce bursts of joy are heard, the piping reed
And tabouret rude at intervals succeed;
The halted tribes in lengthen'd lines are spread,
And in the midst the captive chief is led,
Until he stands before the Sachem's view;
But not, oh! not for clemency to sue.
And as Tekarrah dauntlessly advanc'd,
His eagle eye upon Menana glanc'd;
He gave a quick involuntary start,
And long'd to press the maiden to his heart;
Then lour'd he sternly on the vengeful horde,
Who crav'd his life-blood with one wild accord.
Meanwhile, by pity touch'd, a gentle form,
Apart from all the savage howling swarm,
Restor'd the wretched maid to consciousness;
Ah, cruel kindness! she had felt the less,
If unarous'd from that dull, torpid state,

G 2

To the full horrors of her lover's fate.
The tender damsel then Menana led
From the sad spot, where all seem'd dark and dread;
Nor wish'd Tekarrah to detain her there;
But his eye watch'd her in her deep despair,
Till her lov'd form he could no longer scan;
Then turn'd he calmly round to Simaghan.
Now a brief pause was in their counsels made,
While anxious looks each countenance invade.

END OF CANTO THE SEVENTH.

# MENANA.

## CANTO VIII.

"What Heav'n decrees, no prudence can prevent."
DRYDEN'S AUREN.

ALOFT the Sachem sat, in thought profound,
Elders and chiefs were thickly gather'd round;
They gaz'd upon the captive; he serene
Appear'd with firm and undiscourag'd mien;
Near him the fire-frame stood, erected high,
Ready to light and crimson o'er the sky.
Another shout! Tekarrah, with a smile
Of calm indifference, look'd upon the pile;
Then spoke the Sachem: "Let his breast be bar'd,
"And all the torturing instruments prepar'd.
"Captive! thy fortitude will soon be tried,
"For few have e'er our practis'd skill defied;
"A double vengeance waits thee! From our care
"Thou did'st our daughter artfully ensnare;

" And thou hast won some triumphs o'er our race,
" Which we shall in thy agonies efface;
" Yet, ere the flames surround thee, canst thou show
" What made thee first our nation's deadly foe?
" Speak for thyself, relate thy tale at will,
" Our ears shall listen and our tongues be still."


" What made me first your foe?" the chief replied;
" What made you mine? your nation I defied,
" Because you first cajol'd and then betray'd
" Your faith with ours: those arts *you* first essay'd.
" Some birds build in the forest-trees their nests,
" Whose slaughtering beaks pierce unoffending breasts:
" I strove the remnant of my tribe to shield;
" Would you have had me, like a craven, yield?
" You let not e'en the tree of peace[a] remain,
" But scatter'd wide its honors o'er the plain;
" Ere yet its foliage fully could expand,
" Or its ripe fruits once more endow the land,

---

[a] At a conference held between Francis, Lord Howard of Effingham, Governor-General of His Majesty's dominion of Virginia, and the Chiefs of the Mohawks, Oneydoes, Onnondagas, and Cayagas, in 1684, the spokesman of the Indians gave utterance to the following passage:—"We now plant a tree whose top will reach the sun, and its branches spread far abroad, so that they may be seen afar off; and we shall shelter ourselves under it, and *live in peace* without molestation." Here he gave two beavers. "The Tree of Peace is planted so firmly that it cannot be moved."—*Colden's History of the Five Indian Nations*, vol. i.

" You seiz'd the hatchet, and with ruthless blow
" Laid all its blossoms and its branches low ;
" Our homes were burnt, ourselves like wolves pursu'd,
" Our council-fires extinguish'd in our blood ;
" Our numbers few, yet fewer still remain ;
" Behold these wounds, memorials of your slain.
" Yes, it was thus : from *you* our wrongs arose,
" From hollow friends you grew to deadly foes ;
" By subtle arts our strongest fort was won,
" Our life-blood spilt, and war was thus begun.
" Thick as the leaves that summer-trees put forth,
" Countless as pigeons from the frozen North[a]
" Take their far annual flight to genial skies,
" So numerous would your host our camp surprise.
" Ascend our highest hill, you see no bounds
" To the green regions of our hunting-grounds ;
" They stretch to where the great-head-waters take
" Their rushing course and reach the ' shoreless lake.'[b]
" Those lands were ours, until you lent your aid
" To ' pale intruders,' and our rights betray'd,
" Who through our forest clear'd no friendly path,[c]
" To bring us presents—No ! they came in wrath.

---

[a] On the approach of winter, it is incredible what myriads of pigeons take their flight from the north in a southerly direction, in search of a warmer climate. They literally darken the sky. See *Audubon's account of them in the autumn of* 1813.

[b] The Ocean.

[c] " At last our good father is arrived, he has broken the small branches and cleared his way to meet us."—*Long's Travels*, p. 178.

" Ere we had heard their fire-tubes' thunder roll,
" Few wants we had, and all within control;
" Our game-grounds spread afar on either side,
" And all our foes we dauntlessly defied;
" Our sleep was sound, beneath night's lofty lamp;
" At morn, fat bisons fed around our camp;
" Our tribes now fly before the white-man's pow'r,
" As snows that melt in spring-time's warmer hour;
" You did not e'en our nation's symbol spare,
" Like generous foes—but such you never were;
" The totem-post[a] that mark'd the honor'd grave
" You did not from vile desecration save;
" But fiercely cast it on the trampled mound,
" And strew'd the ashes of the dead around.
" To cairns o'er yonder hills our tribes were led,
" To mourn our fathers in their burial-bed:
" Such visits now we can no more renew,
" And soon the strangers' road will cut them through.

---

[a] *Totem;* The armorial badge or bearing of each tribe into which the various nations are divided. It is the representation of the animal from which the tribe is named. The tribes are named from the eagle, the hawk, the beaver, the buffalo, and from all the beasts of the field, and the fishes of the rivers and lakes. The succession in the tribes is in the female line, and the figure of the sacred animal is the Totem, which every individual of the tribe affixes, whenever his mark is necessary, or whenever he wishes to leave a memorial of himself. This beloved symbol adheres to him in death, and is painted upon the post which marks his grave.—*Remarks on the Condition, Character and Languages of the North American Indians:* Boston, 1826.

" To breathe beneath the shadow of the whites,

" Is to extinguish both our race and rights ;

" We soon shall live in sufferance on the land

" Where we were countless once as grains of sand ;

" Once we were free as dauntless ; but, ah ! now

" The brand of tyranny is on our brow !

" The forests, then our cradles, homes, and graves,

" White men will claim—the red will be their slaves ! "

 

" Son of the woods ! I, not displeas'd, have heard

" Thy death-speech, though thy rage inspir'd each
    word.

" I own thou art well fitted to command,

" And be the leader of a chosen band.

" Food thou should'st have ; but were it giv'n, know—

" That moment we must deem thee friend, not foe."

 

" I ask it not—who can his wants suppress

" Is more of Manitou, of mortal, less.

" Once, when by danger hemm'd on every side,

" I saw the sun in all his cloudless pride

" Seven times sink upon the Salt-lake's tide,

" Ere I or my companions tasted food,[a]

" Save berries gather'd in the straggling wood ;

---

[a] They (the Indians) will traverse forests for hundreds of miles, exposed to the inclemency of the severest weather, and to the pangs of hunger, to gratify their revenge.—*Weld's Travels*. It is well known that the Indians could abstain from food for a remarkable length of time. See *Adair's History of the American Indians*, in

" We cross'd the deer-track—did we halt to eat?

" No; for we only long'd our foes to meet;

" By day and night we followed on their trail,

" Till with our tomahawks we made them quail.

" Squaws [a] may with hunger pine and faint away,

" But warriors patient wait a nobler prey.

" My tale is told—no more have I to say."


The Sachem held his peace, but not unmov'd,

For now his look the multitude reprov'd;

Some gentle feeling in his bosom sprung,

Perchance remembrance of himself when young;

At length he spoke: "Brave warriors, brothers, friends!

" Ignoble means disgrace the noblest ends;

" It may be weakness, nature is but frail,

" And Age is seldom touch'd by woe or wail;

" Yet I confess the captive's tale hath won

" My bosom's ruth; I had myself a son;

" Strange shadowy phantoms crowd upon my mind,

" And point to distant scenes long left behind."

---

which is recorded an almost incredible instance of patience, abstinence, and ingenuity of an Indian in pursuit of his foe, who ran a distance of three hundred computed miles in one day and a half and two nights; and while pursued, threw away his store of barbacued venison and supported nature with herbs, roots, and nuts, which his sharp eyes, with a running glance, directed him to snatch up in his course. —"Their Sachems have been known," says Du Pratz, " to fast for nine days together, eating nothing but maize corn, without meat or fish, and drinking nothing but water, during the whole time."— *History of Louisiana.*      [a] Wives of the Red Indians.

Then turning to Tekarrah, thus pursu'd
The warrior-sage, but in a milder mood:
" Some elder squaws about my camp have said
" Thou wert not born with those thine arm hath led,
" But captur'd by them when thou wert too young
" To tell thy name or from what parents sprung.
" A childless chief adopted thee his own—
" So goes the tale—the truth to me unknown.
" Thou hast no father ! then he will not know
" What 'tis to feel for thee a father's woe.
" For had he liv'd, he soon would have to mourn
" A son who never would to him return ;
" Yet deem thee living still, and still deceiv'd,
" Till both of hope and life himself bereav'd.
" Thou might'st have been an honor to thy sire,
" And in his age renew'd his youthful fire !
" Is the sky bright to thee ? to me 'tis gloom !
" Lovely to thee is yon magnolia's bloom.
" Ah ! all its beauty now to me is dead,
" And every hope I cherish'd long has fled.
" Thou hast no father—had I ne'er been one,
" I had not felt what 'tis to lose a son.
" I had a son, my hope, my joy, my pride !
" Oh, that he'd fallen in battle by my side !
" Unknown his fate; in infancy trepann'd,
" He haply fell into some spoiler's hand;
" Or in some luckless moment chanc'd to stray
" Where the couch'd serpent waits his hapless prey.

" We miss'd him when the season gladness brought
" To all, save me, with grief and anguish fraught;
" When snows had melted in the lake's embrace,
" And birds re-peopl'd every bow'ry place;
" When prairie flowers of purest azure hue
" Disclos'd their tiny blossoms to the view;
" When the young sap through tender branches run,
" And buds to leaves burst forth; I miss'd my son!
" Yes; miss'd him; and I well remember how
" I felt his loss.  I feel it keenly now.
" His mother ow'd to other climes her birth;
" Spain was to her the spirit-home of earth.
" But she was not the first ' pale face' that found
" A peaceful wigwam on our forest ground.
" Not many beaver-moons before, there came
" Men to our shores, from whose cheeks fear or shame
" Seem'd to have scar'd the blood—their skins were
        white,
" And such at first we thought a wondrous sight;
" For we, till then, deem'd all mankind were red.
" From other lands far distant had they sped,
" And hither o'er the great salt waters flew,
" In many a huge and woven-wing'd canoe.
" Each mighty vessel floated o'er the wave,
" As graceful swans their snowy plumage lave;
" Upon their decks there trod a living crowd,
" With faces white as yon light fringe of cloud.

" They came as friends ; alliance, too, they sought,
" And by our side against the Natchez fought.
" But whither leads my memory astray ?
" Why linger thus on scenes long past away ?
" My tender wife, my spirit-dove, is fled,
" And where, my boy, art thou ? to me, ah, dead !
" And now no current of my life-blood flows
" In any human veins[a] of friends or foes !
" Now, left of all my numerous race is none
" To mourn for Simaghan—not one ! not one !
" But truce to thought ! I would this chief had whin'd,
" And, squaw-like, been to coward fears inclin'd ;
" Then had his words have fall'n upon mine ear
" As leaves by " corn-moon" winds are scatter'd sere.
" I fain would save him !"—here a murmur rose—
" And then he added, " but we spare not foes.
" So for the knife his naked breast prepare."
This done, the Sachem starts ; what sees he there ?
" That mark ! Great Spirit ! can it, can it be ?
" My boy ! my long-lost son ! 'Tis he ! 'tis he !"
Then rising from his seat, he faltering stept,
And on Tekarrah's bosom almost wept.

The new-found son appear'd as one amaz'd,
And on the weak and weary warrior gaz'd ;

---

[a] " There runs not a drop of my blood in the veins of any living creature."—*Speech of Logan, a Mingo Chief, to the Governor of Virginia.*

Gleams of astonishment his eye illum'd,
Then it a vague enquiring glance assum'd;
He strove in vain the past to recollect,
No thought could aid him in the retrospect;
Howe'er he tried, he fail'd to bring anew
The vanish'd days of childhood to his view.
His looks oft wander'd o'er the Sachem's face,
As if he there might some remembrance trace,
Some feature stamp'd upon his memory,
Since he had sported round that parent's knee;
Could he have but recall'd a word, a tone,
Or look, he once familiarly had known,
All seeming contradictions then had flown;
But now his mind, bewilder'd and perturb'd,
Became the more perplex'd, the more disturb'd;
'Twas all a chaos; not a single ray
Pierc'd through the veil and chas'd the mist away.
Meanwhile, the throng, amaz'd at what they saw,
Knew not the cause, nor what import to draw.
But quick from mouth to mouth the tidings flew,
Until the wonder universal grew;
But reverence for their vet'ran soon prevail'd,
And shouts of joy the recognition hail'd;
So soon can Nature change the wild desire,
And wean the soul from all its savage ire.

The son led back the father to his seat,
And proud were both thus happily to meet;

Nor needed the old Chieftain to invoke
Attention, while he thus delighted spoke:
" Brothers and children, I am weak and old,
" My brain is frozen, and my blood is cold;
" Yet for your present good and future weal,
" This aged breast can still with ardour feel;
" Nor let my counsel lightly from you go,
" As prints of mocassins dissolve in snow;
" But let the green leaves of your memory,
" When I am gone, my living place supply.
" To all I would the fruits of age impart,
" Then let my words sink deeply in the heart.
" Visit our various tribes from east to west,
" Nor let your feet in sloth indulgent rest,
" Till our red brethren near and far you trace,
" And bind in bonds of peace our scatter'd race.
" Say, from the soul, and not the lips alone,
" How deep the wrongs o'er which we vainly moan.
" Exhort them not to sell their father-land,
" And be your conduct well and wisely plann'd.
" White men would drive us to remoter skies;
" But shall we bid our fathers' bones arise?
" Our fathers, who enjoy'd secure their rights
" For ages, ere they knew the treacherous " whites,"
" Or quaff'd their fire-drink, which can but debase
" Our nations, and our character disgrace.
" Forswear it, and our furs exchange no more
" For the fell draught—the deadly liquid store.

" E'en the war-beverage, drawn from Cassine[a] leaves,

" Drink sparingly—it but the sense deceives.

" Decline the white men's fatal gifts, and tell

" The cheating hucksters that we will not sell

" Of forest, hill, or prairie-ground a thong !

" We will not do our woods and wilds that wrong.

" Shame to our race who would their native soil

" Barter, that white men may their hearths despoil.

" Shall the tall cypress fall beneath their axe,

" That you may in their luxuries relax?

" Or the proud pine, like the poor creeping plant,

" Bend, crouch, and flourish o'er their sordid haunt ?

" Fan not oppression with your living breath,

" But rather moulder in the ' GROVES OF DEATH' ![b]

" Yet speak them gently while you thus deny,

" That still you may nor quarrel nor comply.

" The birds of air, the beasts that range the field,

" The rivers' fish, the fruits the forests yield,

" Were amply given for the red man's use,

" To serve his wants, but not for his abuse.

" The " LORD OF LIFE" said, keep inviolate

" Your hunting grounds in their primeval state ;

" To culture them would frustrate Nature's plan,

" Leave them for herds, for exercise, and man.

" The vigorous chase gives all that we require ;

" The work of squaws would quench our manly fire.

---

[a] The war-drink, an intoxicating liquor drawn from the leaves of the cassine.—*Du Pratz' History of Louisiana.*

[b] The Indians call their cemeteries the " Groves of Death."

" But white men call us savage ; were they right ?

" Why do they tempt us in revenge to smite?

" Speak they to us the voice of love or truth?

" Spare they our wives, our aged, or our youth?

" Shall we our lands, like peltries, put to sale ;

" And when they're ours no more, like infants wail?

" Where are the wigwams, once our fathers' home ?

" The ample prairies, where they lov'd to roam ?

" The plains where feet of strangers never stray'd,

" Till we ourselves our dearest rights betray'd ?

" The white men soon, alas ! will all possess ;

" For, as we still retreat, they forward press.

" Tribes are extinct that once pursu'd the chase,

" Where enemies make now their dwelling place.

" Are not the snows of last year melted down

" To swell the rivers that are overflown ?

" So down Time's stream, into the 'LAKE OF DEATH,'

" Our tribes are hurried to the 'LORD OF BREATH.'

" Our old traditions soon will be forgot,

" For those who cherish'd them are heeded not;

" The songs our fathers lov'd will be unsung,

" And haply soon will die our native tongue.

" The GREAT GOOD SPIRIT taught our race at first

" To keep His laws—we broke them, and are curst.

" The birds and brutes their natures still retain,

" 'Tis only man turns pleasure into pain.

" Without our culture, prairies, woods around,

" With lovely flowers and blushing fruits abound.

" The 'Pale ones' say they might more perfect grow:
" They best know how; the task were hard and slow.
" Scorn their example, spurn their arts, 'twere worse
" To suffer under their enfeebling curse.
" Long, fierce and fiery passions fill'd my soul;
" Now they are tam'd and yield to mild control.
" This truth I've learn'd—better we reconcile
" Our enemies, than bones on bones to pile;
" And let me now in hoary age retire;
" My course is run, and all extinct my fire.
" With me whate'er was bright has had its day,
" And all my honors now are in decay.
" Green trees, fair flowers, and fruits, to me are dead;
" Sun, moon, and stars, have all their lustre shed.
" Elect my son, Tekarrah, as your chief,
" And I shall yield my breath without a grief;
" You know how well his prowess hath been tried,
" What foes have shrunk before him, or have died.
" Yet, listen! 'tis my hope that war may cease,
" And that his bow may henceforth hang in peace;
" Or but be drawn against the flying deer;
" And may the Calumet ᵃ displace the spear!
" Brothers in climate, so as brothers be;
" And curs'd be he who breeds hostility!

---

ᵃ The Calumet, or the Pipe of Peace. Every nation has a
different method of decorating these pipes, so that the tribes to
which they belong are recognized at first sight by these symbols.
They are used as an introduction to all treaties, and great ceremony
attends the use of them on these occasions.

" Let only to the sounds of joy awake

" Savannah, forest, river, wood, and lake;

" Henceforth may every link of Friendship's chain[a]

" Be bright as now, and free from rust or stain;

" Enlarge our love-fires,[b] let them brighter burn,

" Bury the hatchet, nor let war return;

" Your children teach the 'Tree of Peace' to rear,

" Fatal the day that sees its branches bare;

" And war! what is it? full of wild alarms;

" To-day we flourish in successful arms;

" To-morrow, haply, we may fall beneath

" The scalping-knife, or tortur'd be to death.

" Though warriors boast the numbers they have slain,

" Their foes can boast as well, nor boast in vain.

" Then ere my aged bones to earth descend,

" Hear my last pray'r, Great Spirit! and befriend

" Our kindred nations when I am no more

" On earth, but happy on some blissful shore,

" Where I shall meet my sires, and with them share

" The hunter's joy, but not the hunter's care[c];

---

[a] "I will not compare our friendship to a chain; for the rain might sometimes rust it, or a tree might fall and break it."—*W. Penn's Speech to the Indians.*—See *Edinburgh Review on Clarkson's Life of Penn.*

[b] See *Colden's History of the Five Indian Nations*, vol. ii.

[c] "To the wandering Indian, whose eye often followed with desire the rapid flight of the eagle and the deer, it was no doubt sweet to believe that his soul after death should roam through the regions of the air, and over the plains, without ever being wearied."— *Carne's Lives of Eminent Missionaries.* See also *Carver's Travels in the Interior of North America.*

" Root out the Evil Spirit[a] from the breast,
" And let our Indian tribes with peace be blest !
" These thoughts have long within my bosom dwelt,
" In proof of which I give this wampum-belt ! "

The elder chiefs now gave a glad assent,
And the vast throng the air with plaudits rent;
Next they Tekarrah in rich skins array,
And eagles' feathers on his head display;
Then painted for each wound his body bore
As many traces in the tints of gore ;
They arm'd him, too, with arrows, bow, and spear,
The same that former chiefs were wont to bear;
This done, they hail'd him with one loud acclaim,
And all the woods rang with Tekarrah's name.

The son, thus honor'd, now express'd his will
That Simaghan's advice should govern still ;
Whose sagest counsel he would make his guide,
And throw the implements of war aside.
" Let them," he said, " that day commemmorate,
" With peaceful fires and not with flames of hate;
" Let them upon their homeward path return,
" And bid their wives no more their absence mourn;
" Let them revive the embers on each hearth,
" And make their homes again resound with mirth;

---

[a] Arcouski, the Indian God of War.

" Let them at once all injuries forgive,

" And strive in future amity to live;

" So might they smoke the calumet of peace,

" Augment their pleasures, and their cares decrease."

This said, the elders gave assent aloud,

And echo spread their words through all the crowd.


**END OF CANTO THE EIGHTH.**

# MENANA.

---

## CANTO IX.

---

"If power be shewn, and wonderfully so,
  Wonder and thank, adore and bow below."
                                    PARNELL.

---

WHILE for investiture the chiefs conven'd,
Menana by a neighbouring grove was screen'd;
And thus gave vent to feelings deeply ton'd:
" Oh, Thou! above the sun and stars enthron'd,
" Great God of mercy! hear my earnest pray'r,
" And deign my own Tekarrah's life to spare.
" Upon Thy gracious power I still rely;
" But let me cease to hope, if he must die!
" What miracle cannot Thy will perform?
" Can'st thou not in a moment lull the storm?
" Vouchsafe to soften this too savage race,
" And in their breasts some germ of pity place;

" Look with compassion on my deep distress,
" And lead me from this heathen wilderness.
" But not alone; no, let Tekarrah be
" Once more beside me, taught to worship THEE!
" Fain would I seek that resting place, the grave,
" And let the rank weeds o'er my ashes wave,
" If I might dare against Thy law rebel,
" And bid the world and all my griefs farewell.
" Yet, whither shall I seek some lone retreat?
" Whither direct my weak and way-worn feet?
" When the wing'd weary bird inclines to rest,
" She seeks some rocky nook or moss-built nest.
" But I, a hapless wretch, am doom'd to roam,
" Without a guide, protector, friend, or home;
" Save in Thy boundless and benignant care,
" That blessed thought which saves me from despair.
" Yet even now my poor bewilder'd brain
" Is almost madden'd by excess of pain.
" Do I not see before my aching eyes
" The preparation for the sacrifice?
" Must I outlive it? let me now expire,
" Than view the kindling of that ruthless fire!
" Methinks! oh, Heaven! I'm in a dream that blends
" The present, past, and future, but that ends
" Not as a dream; for from this treach'rous sleep
" Reality awakes me but to weep.
" Alas! I do but rave, my senses rock,
" Like the weak vine beneath the tempest's shock.

" At wedding-feasts the married pair receives
" Green, glittering lizards, and dry wither'd leaves : ᵃ
" The first to show how quick existence flies,
" The last to teach how soon each mortal dies.
" Then, patience, 'till this weary life shall cease,
" And my tir'd spirit find eternal peace."


Thus, in the fulness of her bitter woes,
The maid's soliloquies to heaven arose ;
Then from her breast the Sacred Cross she drew,
On which her tears fell fast as evening dew ;
And *that* her mother's latest words recall'd,
Ere her young spirit was as now enthrall'd :
" My daughter ; when the various ills of life
" Shall sore beset thee, care, and grief, and strife,
" Think of the Cross on which the Saviour died,
" For man's redemption basely crucified ;
" And thou wilt find in that most holy sign
" The promise of atonement all divine."

---

ᵃ " Among some tribes, a green lizard, of the species which is
so rapid in its motions that the eye can scarcely follow them, and a
basket-full of dead leaves, intimate to the new-made husband that
time flies and man falls. These people teach in emblems the moral
of life, and indicate by them the part of the labors which nature
has allotted to each of her children."—*Chateaubriand's Travels*,
vol. i, p. 207.

Thus stray'd her thoughts; no friendly sage was
     near,
To whisper soothing counsel in her ear.
Now she bemoan'd her lover's cruel fate,
Now for his rescue Heaven would supplicate;
Gladly she would have yielded up her breath,
Rather than be survivor of his death.
Sometimes a dire temptation half prevail'd,
And Christian fortitude had nearly fail'd.
Would not the mountain-laurel yield a draught,
That, taken once, need never more be quaff'd?
Some potent herbs, that oft diseases heal'd,
But fatal, misapplied, she had conceal'd;
And desperation urg'd, in frantic guise,
By her own act to end her miseries.
But soon the rash suggestion pass'd away,
And meek religion reassum'd its sway.
From her the poison-simples then she cast,
Resign'd to bear and suffer to the last.
" Methinks," she said, " I less with fever burn ;
" And shall I not to Simaghan return?
" Shall not my erring feet their steps retrace,
" And from him importune one last embrace?
" Ungrateful have I been ! Yes, yes, I'll try
" To win forgiveness from him ere I die !
" And these pale, quivering lips shall even yet
" One last chaste imprint on Tekarrah's set;

H

" Impress on his one sadly lingering kiss,
" Sealing two souls in bonds of mutual bliss;
" Of bliss denied on earth to bosoms riv'n,
" But to be fully realiz'd in heaven.
" Yet he shall live! he shall be mine again!
" What can dissever faithful hearts in twain?
" I rave, but am not mad! for still I know
" That I have brought upon myself my woe;
" That I have sinn'd against my mother's creed,
" And for that crime my heart is doom'd to bleed.
" Aid me, great God! for what is now the life
" Thou gav'st, and once with opening blossoms rife?
" A wither'd stem, devoid of flower and fruit,
" Sapp'd at the core—a canker at the root."
Thus to herself the maid apostrophiz'd,
When suddenly a voice her ear surpris'd.

" Ah! cease, my daughter! dry each gushing tear;
" Behold a friend, thy faithful pastor, here;
" Far and fatigu'd my aged feet have sought
" Thy steps, Menana! for my soul is fraught
" Full to o'erflowing with concern for thee,
" And fain would ease thy heart-felt misery.
" Tears ne'er were shed for errors past in vain,
" But only when weak mortals err again,
" Repentance only can efface the stain.
" He, the Great Father, will the proud reprove,
" And raise the meek and lowly by his love;

" The lily bows its leaves and bends its stem,
" To 'scape the storm that rages over them.
" The world has long been dead to me, but yet
" My Heavenly Master bids me not forget,
" Or leave undone the good within my power;
" And He has warn'd me of this trying hour."

As turn'd Menana to the good old man,
Through all her veins surprise and pleasure ran;
But 'twas the flashing of her eye that spoke,
For from her lips scarce half-breath'd murmurs broke;
And when in speech she could articulate,
She strove Tekarrah's perils to narrate;
But, ere she had the painful task essay'd,
The holy pastor check'd the faltering maid.

" My daughter! cease to agonize thy heart,
" I know the narrative thou would'st impart;
" He, who the sinful hath redeem'd below,
" Can mitigate thy bosom's deepest woe.
" I bring thee tidings that may yet revive
" Thy troubled spirit—hope, and pray, and strive
" To bear with meekness, and receive with praise,
" The blessings that may crown thy future days."

" Blessings! Oh, holy father! never more
" Will Heaven upon this head its blessings pour!"

" Rash, impious girl, forbear!" the pastor said,
And with a frown rebuk'd the trembling maid.
" Life is not always stagnant, but at times
" It flows like rapid streams in sunny climes;
" A little rill, through some hard rocky chink,
" Will serve to yield the thirsty traveller drink.
" In Heaven, my child, rely, and place thy trust,
" For God is ever merciful and just.
" Before I met thee here, I mixed among
" The native tribes which these wild forests throng—
" My age and garb protected me from wrong—
" And learn'd from stragglers strange, eventful news
" Which yet thou hast not heard; and I must use
" Discretion, ere my tongue repeats the tale,
" Lest joy, not grief, should o'er thy strength prevail."


" Is dear Tekarrah sav'd? good father, say,
" Tell me *he is*, and I will only pray—
" My joy shall have no vent—nor will I weep—
" But all my senses cool and calmly keep;
" Those words would lend such sweetness to thy voice,
" To hear them, even angels might rejoice!
" Tell me, oh, father! is thy news of him?"


" It is, my child! let tears no longer dim
" Thine eyes; but in thanksgiving bend thy knee,
" And bless the Power that still supporteth thee:

" His life is spar'd!"

                " Oh, God be prais'd!" she cried,
And prostrate sunk the reverend man beside.
In mute devotion there awhile she knelt;
But who can tell what in that space she felt?
The aged pilgrim rais'd his hands on high,
And bow'd his head in hoary sanctity.
At length she rose, with brow serene and clear,
Prepar'd with firmness what remain'd to hear.
The hermit then, with caution, solemn, slow,
Related all the maiden wish'd to know;
How Simaghan had found a long-lost son,
And how Tekarrah had a father won;
How the old chief had closed his honor'd reign,
And of his young successor now how vain!
" And who is *he?*"   Ah, could she not divine?
The good man's eyes proclaim'd him, " He is thine!"

The air by bursts of joyous shouts was rent,
While eager groups in various ways were sent
To seek Menana; some their footsteps bend
To where they find her with her ancient friend.
Urged on by words full of kind feeling fraught,
To Simaghan they both were quickly brought.

### END OF CANTO THE NINTH.

# MENANA.

## CANTO X.

"Not a sister, scarce a brother."
POEMS BY JOHN HALL, 1648.
"Now warm in love, now withering in the grave."
DRYDEN.

BESIDE his hoary sire Tekarrah sate,
Array'd in all th' insignia of his state.
But when the dusky throng dividing drew
Apart, and show'd Menana to his view,
His feelings burst the bonds of all control,
And ardent passion seiz'd his inmost soul.
Rushing, at once he clasp'd her to his breast,
And to her lips his own with fervor press'd.
More calmly next the hermit he embrac'd,
And kiss'd the cross suspended from his waist;

Then drew it from his tunic reverently,
And held it as a symbol from on high;
While Simaghan look'd on in dreamy thought,
And it might be some change was in him wrought.
He now broke silence, and Menana's name
From his parch'd lips in trembling cadence came.
Tekarrah bore her to the old man's side,
And not untenderly the maid he ey'd;
He took her hand and kiss'd her pallid cheek,
And presently he thus began to speak:


" Poor, hapless child!   Menana, thou hast come,
" Ere my tir'd spirit seek its viewless home.
" We should not with our dying breath retain
" One feeling that might give another pain.
" Take my forgiveness, for the troth I bore
" Her who convey'd thee to the Red Man's shore;
" Yea, let me in these feeble moments own,
" My heart's deep yearnings are for thee alone!
" When death had snatch'd thy mother from my view,
" Thou didst her presence to my mind renew;
" When stretch'd and wounded on my mat I lay,
" 'Twas thine to wile the tedious hours away;
" Nor do I blame thee, that in utmost need
" Thou didst Tekarrah's cause so boldly plead:
" But never can'st thou hope to be his bride—
" Sister and brother are too near allied;

" Give heed! a band of warriors once I led
" To the broad margin of the ' Salt-Lake's bed' ;
" Upon the beach we found a huge canoe,
" Which had been left there when the waves withdrew ;
" Three ' Whites ' were lying senseless on the deck,
" The sole survivors of a fatal wreck ;
" They by the ruthless billows had been spar'd,
" While all the rest a watery grave had shar'd ;
" Thyself and mother, lock'd in close embrace,
" Seem'd as if death had clasp'd both face to face ;
" The third, 'The Great Good Spirit's Man,' a priest ;
" When from his perils he had been releas'd,
" Soon wander'd from us, and we know not where,
" Nor since have seen that aged ' chief of pray'r' ;
" No other living beings were on board,
" But those we rescu'd, and to strength restor'd.
" Thyself and mother to our camp were brought,
" Our arts, our customs, and our language taught.
" After a while, a tender feeling grew
" Within my breast I could not well subdue ;
" I sought your mother's love, but long in vain ;
" At length she yielded, though with secret pain ;
" Not love, but gratitude, impell'd consent,
" Yet never did she murmur discontent ;
" She gave Tekarrah birth, my only boy ;
" My long, long lost, but now recover'd joy ;
" He was the playmate of thy infant love,
" Like the young eagle he, and thou the dove."

"Tekarrah!" faintly gasp'd the startled maid,
"Tekarrah! said'st thou? oh, what thoughts invade
"My agitated soul! what tumults rise
"Within my breast! and there what horror lies!"

"Both of one mother!" from Tekarrah burst.
"Oh! from my birth my doom has been accurst!
"But just redeem'd from an inglorious death,
"Command and power now hang upon my breath;
"Yet what is fame or honor to me now,
"Since cruel fate annuls each dearest vow?
"With thee, Menana! all my hopes are lost,
"And I win greatness at too great a cost.
"Methinks I dream, and yet I am awake!
"Must I my love, my cherish'd love forsake?
"My soul's pure idol, my affianc'd bride?
"Yet should I spurn a sister from my side?
"'Master of Life!' what changes hast thou wrought!
"With what dark ills my destiny is fraught!"

"Cease," said the Sachem, "to repine at fate;
"Good, when it comes at all, is ne'er too late;
"The *flower* of manhood thou hast scarcely known;
"On me the *snows* of wintry age are strown;
"Thy future days will brighten in the sun;
"But mine, ah! mine are like my fathers', done!
"Weep not, Menana, like the dappled doe,
"'Tis only to a distant land I go!"

Sweetness was in the tones with which he spoke,
Like new-found honey in an ancient oak.


" Once I was stout of limb and firm in frame,
" Keen was my vision, true in taking aim;
" As o'er my head the eagle, soaring past,
" Took higher range, lest it might prove his last;
" And now he mocks me in his lazy flight,
" My arm is nerveless grown, and dim my sight;
" Why should I grieve at age?   I've had my time
" Of youth and bravery—my spring and prime;
" I'm like a sycamore whose boughs once spread,
" And shaded many.—Now I'm wither'd, dead!
" Now, like the oak-moss, where the sun has shone,
" My hair is white and all its sap is gone;
" Nor can I curve, as I was wont, the bow,
" Nor wield, as once, my axe with deadly blow;
" My tree of life is now for ever bent,
" Its honors in decay—its branches rent;
" My trembling limbs refuse the eager chase,
" And soon will moulder in their burial-place.
" It had been pain to die ere life was dull,
" While all my veins were in their vigour full;
" But when the strength to wield the axe is past,
" It matters not how soon I breathe my last;
" And now, my friends, companions, brethren all,
" Soon shall my spirit quit its earthly thrall;

" Adieu, ye lakes, ye woods, ye prairies green,
" Each long-remember'd and familiar scene !
" Yet in this hour it glads my heart to know
" My son will not disgrace his father's bow.
" And, brethren, may his rule be wise as brave,
" In battle valiant, and in council grave."

This effort made, his voice became so weak,
That, sinking on his couch, he ceas'd to speak.
But on his son awhile he fix'd his eyes,
Then turn'd them upward to the glowing skies.
His life-pulse feebler grew, yet life was *there ;*
Still had not come the moment of despair.
To speak again he rallied now his strength,
And thus his parting words resum'd at length,
So that tradition might preserve his name,
As not unworthy of his former fame.

" Methinks yon sun, now setting in the West,
" Is like my sire, this earth my mother's breast.
" Raise, raise me up! it yet my bosom thrills
" To see his brightness rest on yonder hills !
" Undazzl'd by his splendour, let me gaze
" Till sullen darkness shroud his gorgeous blaze.
" Say, shall I not be borne to some bright star
" Where all my fathers' blissful spirits are ?
" Where ample foliage casts a welcome shade
" O'er the smooth lake, and every forest glade

" Is peopled with the sportive, lusty deer,
" Where bisons rush upon the hunter's spear,
" And summer reigns through all the happy year ?
" There shall I through the flowery prairies roam,
" And the oak's foliage there shall make my home ;
" There shall I listen to some chieftain's tale,
" Join'd with the music of the breezy gale.
" Of acts of prowess done in days of yore,
" Ere white men's feet were trac'd upon our shore.
" Such deeds as were achiev'd when yon old trees
" Were saplings scarcely higher than my knees.
" No proofs of valour in these scars you see,
" Save what belong to foes and not to me.
" Not time alone hath turn'd this hair so light,
" Care, too, hath chang'd its raven hue to white.
" Too heedless youth would noble toil forsake ;
" Age must the watch-fire's embers keep awake.
" But would you know the feats these arms have done,
" Go, ask what hostile race hath lost a son,
" A father, husband, brother, chieftain brave,
" And whose the might that laid him in the grave."

    He paus'd a little while in silence ;  then,
Still pointing to the West, resum'd again.
" Yes, that bright sun, in all its fiery state,
" I ever deem'd the guardian of my fate.
" Thou radiant orb ! Creation's golden light !
" Exhale my latest breath ! I sink in night !

" I sink—but not to rise again, O, Sun !
" Again like thee my daily course to run.
" God of Eternal Fire ! thy rays shall shed
" No more their lustre on this living head !
" Yet do I still thy presence hail, and bend
" In joy before thee, as we both descend.
" Farewell, kind warmth ! effulgent light, farewell !
" I only go to where my fathers dwell !''

Unnotic'd had the reverend hermit stood,
Spectator of the scene, in silent mood ;
But now beside the dying chief he bent,
And freely gave his soul's emotions vent,
Avow'd himself the aged man of pray'r
Found on the wreck in motionless despair.
The Sachem seem'd a moment to revive
At this, and with his memory to strive ;
Then, when the priest's brief narrative was done,
He sunk with still his eyes fix'd on the sun—
Those eyes fast glazing—and on *that* alone,
As though their sense had to it firmly grown.
One arm he feebly pointed to the West,
The other lay in stillness on his breast.
Around him pensive stood each elder chief,
Not without feeling, but with stifled grief;
While all appear'd to wait, with anxious eye,
Some more than usual signal from the sky,

Until the sun's last parting rays were shed;
Then came a groan—and Simaghan was dead.


The crowd awhile were struck with awe profound,
And their late chieftain's relics gather'd round.
At length, a warrior of superior sway
Gave orders that they should be borne away.
Wrapt then in ermine-furs, the corse was plac'd
In a deep valley's lone and lovely waste,
Where with rich feathers it was duly dress'd,[a]
Ere shrin'd within a curious cane-wrought [b] chest.
Thence 'twas remov'd with slow funereal train,
In the " great village " to awhile remain:
Till to the rude pil'd cairn at last convey'd,
To rest in peace beneath the silent shade.
Loud was the wail, and far around it spread
The piercing lamentation for the dead;
For old and young, commingling near the spot,
In this one sorrow minor griefs forgot.

---

[a] " We entered the hut of the deceased, and found him on his
bed of state, dressed in his finest clothes, his face painted with
vermilion, shod as if for a journey, *with his feather-crown on his
head.*"—*Hist. of Louisiana*, p. 354.

[b] " In the largest apartment the eternal fire is kept, and there
is likewise a table or altar in it, about four feet high, six long, and
two broad.  On this table lie the bones of the Great Sun, *in a coffin
of canes, very neatly made.*"—Ibid. p. 351.

Thus paid the honors at the moment due,
The mournful throng in various ways withdrew;
All, save Tekarrah, who, half-paralys'd,
Seem'd brooding still, and thus soliloquis'd:


" And have I lost as soon as found a sire,
" For whom my heart confess'd its filial fire ?
" But the GREAT SPIRIT did not life bestow
" To linger on eternally below;
" And age is sure the brightest eye to dim,
" Check the fleet foot, and strain the active limb;
" The mighty oak itself must yield to time,
" And lose the verdant glories of its prime.
" Then wherefore should I pine for Simaghan ?
" Although my father, yet he was but man.
" Oh ! rather let me turn my thoughts to one
" Who, like myself, hath been by love undone.
" Menana ! art thou here ? to thee I bend,
" No more a lover, but a brother, friend;
" Yet shall I chiefly still exist for thee,
" And thou my light, my constant star shall be,
" My sweet instructress in the ' Great Good Word,ᵃ'
" Which from thy lips I've oft too heedless heard;
" Thou shalt confirm me in the Christian's creed,
" And elevate my soul to joy indeed !

---

ᵃ The Scriptures.

" Nor evermore be sever'd from my side,
" My earthly teacher, and my heavenly guide!"


" Too late, Tekarrah! oh, 'tis now too late
" To cherish hope, and vain to war with fate.
" Soon must this frame resign its fleeting breath,
" I feel within me now the pangs of death.
" But when my spirit here no more shall dwell,
" Oh, let not thine against God's will rebel,
" To whose pure worship now thou art inclin'd.
" HE fails not ever to enrich the mind
" With light and love, and happiness supreme,
" And fill the soul with truth's eternal beam.
" Oh! fatal day, when thou first won my heart!
" Had we not lov'd, 'twere now no pain to part!
" My earliest sorrow was thy death to fear,
" My latest one is now to leave thee here;
" But we shall meet, yes, in a world of bliss,
" With purer love than we have known in this;
" A pure, an endless love shall then be ours
"To re-unite our souls in heavenly bow'rs!
" Oh, shed no tear! let no deep grief be thine;
" Some happier star may o'er thy future shine.
" And when I'm gone, deem not a hasty death
" Assail'd my frame and yielded heaven my breath;
" Ah, no! my health declin'd on that sad day
" I saw thee go to hunt the forest-prey:

" Thy brief farewell, the parting on that morn,
" Left my poor heart faint, joyless, and forlorn.
" My life is ebbing through each frozen vein,
" My strength no longer can that life sustain;
" Bewildering feelings o'er my senses creep;
" But grieve not! I conjure thee not to weep!
" Think, when my breath has fled, I sleep.—Forget
" 'Tis death, and say ' she has not risen yet.'
" Think that I have a respite from my woes,
" That sorrow would but break my sweet repose."

At this he rais'd his eyes which met her own,
While hers with more than wonted sweetness shone;
His anguish now betray'd the prison'd tear,
Long check'd and hidden in his lids, from fear
The sad bereavement of his wounded heart
To hers might all its poignancy impart.
Yet on Menana could he look unmov'd,
Nor dread to lose the dear one so much lov'd?
Oh, no! he knew the final hour was near!
Her last on earth—that time of mournful fear,
The last in life that she could with him stay,
And that no sorrow could redeem the day
On which the soul for ever wings its way.
Her panting frame might soon resign its breath,
And her mild angel-eyes be clos'd in death;
Turn then he could not from those gentle orbs,
Now fix'd on him; and memory, which absorbs

The soul, recall'd each past and present theme,
While, in abstraction lost as in a dream
Of grief's abandonment, his fancy stray'd
O'er hours of pleasure past with his lov'd maid.
Yes, on her features, as in spell-bound trance,
He gaz'd, as if he liv'd but on her glance.
She, mov'd with pity, gently press'd his hand,
And said, with voice too faltering to command,
" Tekarrah ! soon—nay—in a little hour—
" Thou wilt behold me a poor wither'd flow'r ! "
She paus'd a moment, and in languid tone,
Of very sweetness, call'd him " her dear own !"
To heav'n her eyes soon rais'd in silent pray'r,
As if her spirit were ascending there;
Then on his ear her parting accent fell,
" My own Tekarrah—brother—love—farewell !"
Her tremulous lips essay'd once more to speak—
Without avail—her voice was now too weak.
In sighs the anguish of her soul was past;
Upon Tekarrah one fond look she cast,
One gaze of tenderness—it was her last !

Nearer he stoop'd to catch another breath,
As if he doubted whether this was death.
Too surely had the soul obtain'd release,
And on her features settled perfect peace.
Now in his arms he rais'd her lifeless form,
Tried the fix'd pulse while yet the veins were warm;

Then the dear corse of one so lov'd he press'd
Closer and closer to his aching breast.
His eyes still gaz'd upon her pallid brow,
Until he felt convinc'd 'twas painless now.
But, though eclips'd in death, her angel-face
Retain'd its sweet, expressive, living grace.
Tekarrah's sorrows it were vain to tell,
As to her lov'd remains he bade farewell.

Through many weary leagues of forest track
They bore the corse of poor Menana back,
To bury her within her mother's grave,
A mound beside the Mississippi's wave,
Nam'd, by the natives there of sun-born blood,
The lone White Stranger's Cairn beside the
     flood;
But other tribes, that view'd the spot with awe,
Call'd it The Grave of Simaghan's White Squaw.
Beneath their burthen silently they went,
With looks of woe most sadly eloquent.
The Hermit solemniz'd the funeral-rite,
With Christian forms, at the still hour of night;
Then dropp'd a tear upon the dust below,
The last that from his eyes might ever flow.
Facing the rising sun they laid her head,
Pil'd up the earth upon her burial-bed,
And scattering pebbles o'er the narrow mound,
Left it with many a look of grief profound.

From that day forth the monk no more was seen,
Save in his lone retreat ; but, times between,
Oft would Tekarrah with the good man spend
The evening hour, and to his converse lend
A willing ear and most attentive mind ;
Though what the theme, was to themselves confin'd.
Enough to know, the Chief at length became
A convert to the Cross—the Saviour's name !


One summer's eve, he went to greet the sage
As usual in his rural hermitage ;
The old man, mostly at the wonted hour,
Receiv'd him at the entrance to his bow'r ;
But now he came not forth, no voice was heard,
No footsteps from the rocky cloister stirr'd.
Tekarrah enter'd, not without some dread
That he might find his Christian pastor dead.
Ah ! what beheld he ? at the altar there
A figure knelt, as in the act of pray'r.
But he had breath'd to Heav'n his latest sigh,
And his pure spirit had been borne on high.
The spot he hallow'd with his living breath
Became his fittest resting place in death.
Tekarrah mourn'd him as a grateful son
Would mourn a father and true friend in one ;
And cherish'd in his heart a hope sincere
Again to meet him in a happier sphere.

After long years, an aged pilgrim came
To poor Menana's grave ; weak was his frame,
And weary seem'd his feet ; the dress he wore
To that of Indian tribes some semblance bore.
His once athletic form emotion shook,
Furrow'd his cheek, and woe-worn was his look.
His fount of sorrow had been dried for years ;
But now he wept, nor sought to check his tears.
A pause he made, then turn'd his steps aside
To where a rock o'erlook'd the foaming tide ;
A massy fragment of the fallen stone,
With crimson lichen [a] and green moss o'ergrown,
He brought, with labour, to her lonely bed,
And on it, as a pillow, laid his head ;
Then rais'd his eyes to Heav'n with pious grief,
And died !—he was the Natchez-Indian Chief.


Some followers watch'd his footsteps to the mound,
Then nearer to his breathless corse drew round.
His grave they dug beside Menana's, where
They laid his body with observant care.
His bow, his arrows, and the cross she wore,
His mocassins and things of household store,

---

[a] Mention is made of such lichen in Mrs. Trail's *Buckwoods of Canada.*

They buried with him, that he might not be
A restless spirit, haunting hut and tree,[a]
Things he in life had lov'd unspeakably.
Two simple cairns alone the spot reveal,
And thither often youths and maidens steal
To sigh o'er hapless love, or whisper vows,
Like the fond myrtle's intertwining boughs.


　　Years follow'd years before that tale of grief
Of the White Maiden and the Indian Chief
Ceas'd to engage the Red Girl's thoughts, or move
Her heart to melt at poor Menana's love.
Oft it beguil'd the hunter's weary way,
Returning from the chase at close of day ;
And o'er the camp-fire warriors would relate
Tekarrah's exploits and unhappy fate.
Still many a spot, in each adjacent grove,
Retain some sad memorial of their love ;
In simple beauty on each hallow'd tomb,
The everlasting love-flow'r[b] sheds its bloom ;

---

[a] It is believed that unless these articles be buried with the body, the spirit of the deceased will appear among the trees near his lodge or wigwam, and does not go to rest till the property withheld be committed to the grave.—*Lardner's Western World*, vol. i.

[b] Gnaphalium or Cudweed, I believe.

And virgins deem Menana's spirit there
Hovers at twilight in the balmy air;
Or, when above the spot the night-winds blow,
They seem a dirge for those who sleep below.
Though many a native tribe has pass'd away
Since the events that form this simple lay,
Yet still the record shall not wholly fade
Of the RED INDIAN and the SOUTHERN MAID.

END OF THE TENTH AND LAST CANTO OF MENANA.

It has been said that the *sentiment* of love is almost wholly unknown among the Indian tribes; but this assertion has been contradicted by all the best authorities on the subject, and scarcely needs further refutation. Indeed, it is manifest that the feelings of nature must be everywhere alike; of course differently modified according to place and circumstances. Chateaubriand, who was well acquainted, from personal intercourse, with the Indian character, entertained a contrary opinion to that above alluded to, or his beautiful tale of ATALA had never been written. The many interesting facts and traditions embodied in the numerous works that have treated of the manners and customs of the Indians, by writers of unquestionable veracity, are all opposed to the idea that they are unsusceptible of the tenderest impressions. Their very language, abounding as it does in most touching and natural images and forms of expression, affords ample proof that their hearts cannot be insensible to many of the finest emotions, as well as to the most vehement passions. An able writer, speaking of these uncultured tribes, says that "no people on earth are more alive to the calls of friendship; no people have a greater affection for their offspring in their tender years; no people are more sensible of an injury."

Colonel Lee, a gentleman who has resided with the Red Indians for a considerable period, and who has twice since volunteered again to sojourn amongst them, if by so doing any beneficial object could be promoted, was kind enough to inform the author, that those specimens of the Indian tribes of North America who have been brought to and exhibited in this country have been of a degenerate or spurious breed. The Red man whose blood is preserved uncontaminated, is far too high-spirited to suffer himself to be made a show of; nor could he be easily induced to quit his native wilds and forests by any temptation of a mercenary nature.

Tekarrah's expressions of warmth for Menana, differing (as some would erroneously say) from the regard which the Red Indians generally evince to the other sex of the native tribes, is accounted for in the sequel—his mother having been a native of the Sunny South, a Spanish woman.

# THE DEATH ROBE.

## I.

'TWAS where the Mississippi proudly flows
　　Through forests planted when the world was new,
Whose giant trees in stately grandeur rose,
　　Unchang'd by man since from their birth they grew,
Some Indians crowded on the bank, to view
　　A sight such as they ne'er had seen before—
A steam-ship, called by them a " Fire-Canoe,"
　　Which, oarless, sailless, as it near'd the shore,
　　Smoking and whizzing, rais'd their wonder more
　　　　and more.

## II.

They mark'd with what velocity and force,
　　Urg'd by her fiery breath, each paddle wheel
Smote the strong foaming waters on her course,
　　And with what stedfastness she kept her keel;
They almost thought that she could see and feel,
　　And, like a living thing, could hear and speak;
Some said 'twas MIC-HA-BOU,[a] whose wrath to deal,
　　Had thither from his Cataract come; all seek
　　The mystery to solve by fancies wild and weak.

---

[a] Mic-ha-bou, the god of the waters, is said to reside in the Cataract of St. Anthony.

I

### III.

The " wing'd canoes " [a] wafted from distant skies,
    Across the surface of the " shoreless lake,"
No longer rais'd within their minds surprise,
    Though *they*, at first, like wonder did awake :
But of this monster nothing could they make ;
    Against both wind and tide it forc'd its way,
As though it could through strongest barriers break ;
    If for a time they felt, perchance, dismay,
    Their fears were soon dispell'd by reason's better
        sway.

### IV.

The traders landed, natives gather'd round,
    And packages were rang'd in goodly row ;
To seek a mart the vessel had been bound,
    And now her crew to barter were not slow,
But spread their wares, as best they could, for show.
    Red men of wampum-belts exchanges made,
Pledges of present troth for weal or woe,
    Ere they their peltries on the sward display'd ;
    For now they sought to share the mutual gains of
        trade.

### V.

Around them crowds of painted warriors stood,
    Groups, too, of women mingled, young and old ;
And children issued playful from the wood,
    And stragglers here and there unheeded stroll'd.
Anon, upon the broad and winding river roll'd
    A light birch-shallop, now more plainly seen ;
From which an Indian Chief, of aspect bold,
    With limb athletic and with fearless mien,
    In a strange vesture clad, stepp'd forth upon the
        green.

---

[a] Sailing vessels.

## VI.

Behind a grassy knoll near lay conceal'd
   A human figure, that with restless eye
Minutely scann'd what objects were reveal'd
   Unto his eager gaze, impatiently.
His skin bespoke him of a different sky,
   His garb was that of Europe's paler race :
He keenly watch'd a maid of darker dye,
   Who tripp'd along with nature's matchless grace ;—
In Cameron's heart she held an undivided place.


## VII.

And now he quickly sprung from his retreat ;
   The Red maid met him with a startled look :
He seiz'd her hand, and led her to a seat
   Upon a bank, beside a gentle brook ;
And as he spoke, his frame with tremor shook :
   "Hast thou," he said, "thy love to Morah sworn ?
" Doth he not lurk in every covert nook ?
   " Is he not of a base-bred nature born ?
   "Hold then his peltries, steeds, and him in utter
       scorn !


## VIII.

" I know he doth in me a rival fear ;
   " Jealous he is thou should'st go forth alone ;
" Though he is rich, yet he shall buy thee dear ;
   " For this I swear, thou soon shalt be mine own.
" Till now, my heart no love hath ever known ;
   " But since I feel its power, I will defy
" His most seductive, or most daring tone ;
   " His gifts I may by richer ones outvie ;
   " Plight but thy troth to me, and we afar will fly.

## IX.

" In ' Fire-Canoe,' like that we now behold,
  " Some six moons since, I visited the shore,
" Where, distant hence, yon restless river roll'd,
  " And hither came these wild woods to explore,
" For herbs medicinal unknown before,
  " As health is valued more than peltries rare ;
" 'Twas then I first beheld thee to adore,
  " And I besought thee in brief space to share
    " My hand, my heart, my home, nor didst thou me
        forswear.

## X.

" Four wives already share the Chief's embrace,
  " And wilt thou add another to his pride ?
" My Forest Maid should ne'er consent to grace
  " His hateful wigwam, and his love divide :
" The white men only take a single bride,
  " And then true happiness is either's lot ;
" Such is the custom o'er the ' Great salt tide,'
  " And we may hasten thither, here forgot ;
  " Better, perchance, to be by foes remember'd not.

## XI.

" My proud Red rival, from that trader's store
  " Struts in the brightness of a gaudy cloak ;
" Lately, the bison's thong-bound hide he wore,
  " Which, simply rude, no vanity bespoke ;
" His garb may now the Spirit's wrath provoke ;
  " To no false trappings should a chief be prone ;
" To the light breeze ne'er bends the sturdy oak ;
  " And Morah now hath self-conceited grown ;
  " An omen that his pride will soon be overthrown.

### XII.

" Shun the Chief's presence! do not near him come.
  " And hear my words:—within that ' fire-canoe,'
" That rais'd thy wonder as it rous'd the foam,
  " A white man, lingering of the plague-spot,[a] drew
" That cloak around him, Morah's pride may rue:
  " So now, beware! take heed unto thy health!
" Lest he may thee in that same garment woo,
  " Nay, press his passion—bear thee off by stealth!
  " But, oh! forbid it, Heav'n! Thou'rt more to me
      than wealth!

### XIII.

" The sufferer soon of the contagion died;
  " While dying, he that tainted garment wore;
" His corse was plung'd from off the vessel's side
  " Into the waves below; _his_ pains were o'er,
" But woe the hour that brought him to this shore.
  " Morah beheld the ' fire-ship' from the steep,
" And to the water's edge some peltries bore,
  " Then sprung on board the bark with eager leap,
  " And bought the baneful cloak which he doth
      proudly keep."

### XIV.

" Thy words have fill'd my bosom with alarm!"
  Replied the Red maid. " Can, indeed, disease
" In a worn woollen vestment work such harm,
  " That frightful death shall on the wearer scize?
" But broken vows might MANITOU displease,
  " And for a ' Pale Face' to forsake my race;
" Yet, I must fain confess, my heart 't would ease,
  " If my white lover were in Morah's place;
  " But I may not my father's honor'd name disgrace.

---

[a] The small-pox.

## XV.

" The people of the unsunn'd land are wise,
  " Wise, too, is Cameron, and quick of sight ;
" But doth he know what arts the Red Man tries,
  " When he suspects a wrong, or claims a right ?
" Need I confess I would thy love requite ?
  " Though I may not that feeling show, alas !
" A word, a look might our love-meetings blight.
  " Ha ! " whisper'd she, " behold yon moving grass,
  " Like a black snake, conceal'd, *he* lists what now
      may pass ! "

## XVI.

This said, she flew to an adjacent wood ;
  And Cameron would have track'd her flying feet ;
When suddenly the chief before him stood,
  And thus accosted him with words discreet :
" White Brother ! as by chance alone we meet,
  " Deeds worthy of myself I fain would show ;
" For friendship is as forest-honey sweet ;
  " The GREAT GOOD SPIRIT gave the hunter's bow
  " To the Red Men—to the ' Whites,' the arts we
      little know.

## XVII.

" Of land we've plenty ; therefore freely take
  " Whate'er thou wilt, and use our hunting-ground,
" Thy wattled hut here unmolested make,
  " Where bisons graze, and herds of deer abound.
" Our tribe in thee a faithful friend hath found,
  " And would as brother gladly hail thee too ;
" Worthy our virgins are ; then look around,
  " And little labour need'st thou take to woo ;
  " Excepting STAR-FLOWER, choose ; but bid to
      her adieu."

### XVIII.

" Morah ! my courtesy and thanks are due,
  " But yet I must thy tempting words withstand ;
" In sooth, I'm like a drifted, lost canoe,
  " Forc'd by the waves upon a barren strand,
" Without a partner of my heart and hand,
  " —And only woman lends a charm to life ;—
" Her smile can fertilize a sterile land,
  " And e'en disarm the savage breast of strife ;
  " Yet I from *thee* can ne'er accept that gift—a wife.

### XIX.

" 'Tis woman's chaste and undivided love,
  " Bestow'd on one who gives her his alone,
" That constitutes the bliss 'Whites' only prove,
  " Which never can be to the Red Men known,
" Who a plurality of spouses own ;
  " Thou claimest STAR-FLOWER ; STAR-FLOWER *I*
        would wed ;
" A mutual passion in our breasts have grown ;
  " Morah, the maid regards thee but with dread,
  " Ere she should link with thee, I would behold
        her dead.

### XX.

" My first, my last, my fondest, dearest thought,
  " From morning's dawn to evening's dewy close,
" Is fix'd on her ; nor can I e'er be brought
  " Her image to resign e'en in repose ;
" For when at day's decline, fatigu'd, I doze,
  " Her presence still I in my visions feign ;
" A thousand raptures then my spirit knows ;
  " Soft music seems to captivate my brain,
  " Until I wake to stern reality again.

## XXI.

" Red Chief! thou know'st not what it is to love—
  " Love can inhabit no such breast as thine;
" It is a flame that comes from heaven above,
  " And only gentle hearts will it enshrine,
" Though often ruder natures 'twill refine :
  " But 'tis resistless as a mountain-stream,
" No feeble barrier can its course impede;
  " Then think not I persuasive words esteem,
" Or that thy strongest arguments may plead;
" Like vision'd things in dreams, of them I take no
      heed ! "

## XXII.

" There is much wisdom," spake the crafty Chief,
  " In all the words my rival now doth say;
" That he the STAR-FLOWER loves is our belief,
  " But she hath wrongly led his heart astray.
" The hunter never claims his brother's prey :
  " Two steeds, as fair in form as fleet in chase,
" To WAR-BIRD, STAR-FLOWER's father, I did pay,
  " That she in me a husband should embrace;
  " Let him at once decide whose wigwam she shall
      grace."

## XXIII.

In three days hence the suitors now agreed
  To visit ' War-bird,' and together go;
Anxious were they to prove who would succeed
  To bear Star-flower from home, for weal or woe;
  But he who could the costliest gifts bestow,
Would by her sordid sire be undenied,
  Nor to his daughter's feelings would he show
The smallest preference, beyond what pride
And avarice might prompt him, unto either side.

### XXIV.

On the appointed day, the rival pair,
   To the maid's dwelling, hid by shrub and tree,
Came—each his earnest passion to declare;
   And ' War-bird,' rising, smil'd the twain to see;
   While he, with manner unconstrain'd and free,
Welcom'd them both; but ere they could proceed
   To make their business known, or urge their plea,
He proffer'd them the pipe of odorous weed,
The fragrant smoke they drew as if in friendly deed.

### XXV.

Then Morah spoke, and Cameron was mute;—
   " My brother and myself have both one aim
" (We meet for right, and brief be the dispute),
   " To win thy daughter's hand—our suit the same—
   " But mine thou must admit the prior claim;
" She's mine betroth'd; to wed her now I seek;
   " Nor canst thou justly my impatience blame;
" Thy judgment must decide whose cause is weak,
" And Morah will in peace now hear his white friend
        speak."

### XXVI.

In gentle accents Cameron thus replied:
   " Love should be ever mutual and free.
" Woe to the man who would those hearts divide
   " That have been knit in faith and purity.
   " The maiden and myself in this agree—
" That we are bound together by a chain
   " No human power can break; then cautious be
" How thou wouldst seek to separate us twain,
" Lest such attempt should prove as dangerous as
        vain."

### XXVII.

" Let the White Trader hear and understand,"
　　Said STAR-FLOWER's father, "that 'twould be my pride
" To have the Stranger from the far-off land
　　" To me and mine by kindred ties allied;
　　" But I, perforce, must by my pledge abide;
" STAR-FLOWER may not with the white man unite,
　　" But Morah must possess her as his bride;
" He justly claiming her by prior right—
" And thus I now decide, nor seek my will to slight."


### XXVIII.

" Thy words upon mine ear right welcome fall,"
　　Exclaim'd the Red Chief, " Peace to thee and thine!
" If for thy daughter were my gifts too small,
　　" They shall be multiplied to make her mine.
　　" Let my white brother his pretence resign,
" Since he must own no chance doth now remain;
　　" And round him let as sweet a tendril twine
" As STAR-FLOWER is, but her not hope to gain :—
" Of what injustice can my white friend now complain ?"


### XXIX.

" 'Tis the GOOD SPIRIT's Will she shall be mine!"
　　Cameron rejoin'd, " for so it is decreed;
" The grave will have a victim ere she's thine;
　　" That victim thou !—so to my words give heed!
　　" Discard that cloak, if not too late, indeed!
" It bears about it pestilence and death :
　　" Through villages it may infection breed!—
" An unseen danger lurks within thy breath
" To many! Morah, mark what thy white brother
　　　　　saith!"

### XXX.

" The Stranger speaketh well; for he is wise;
  " And we would on his warning fain rely,
" But that to mortals MANITOU denies
  " The knowledge of events to come; and why
  " Should white men have the gift of prophecy
"And not the 'Red-skin?' Why should things unknown,
  " When secret kept in dark futurity,
" Be to my pale-fac'd brother's vision shown?
" Why should *his* nation be more favor'd than my
      own?

### XXXI.

" 'Tis not for man the future to unfold;
  " *That* knowledge is to MANITOU confin'd;
" Though Sachems,ᵃ it is said, may have foretold
  " Of things that came to pass; but we are blind
  " To our own destiny; such is my mind;
" But when the earth is parch'd by heats most dire,
  " And neither man nor beast can water find,
" And both for want of drink too oft expire,
" Such fatal signs as these bespeak HIS awful ire.

### XXXII.

" But since the far-off comers we descried
  " In wing'd canoes along our forest-shore;
" Since, to the daughters of our chiefs allied,
  " They claim'd whatever land they might explore,
  " Ruling us as we ne'er were rul'd before;
" To them the spreading plague-spot first we trace,
  " With other ills our sires knew not of yore;
" Yet we these ' Whites ' with open arms embrace,
" While still they bay and hunt the remnant of our
      race."

---

ᵃ Elders of the tribe.

### XXXIII.

"Hold! hold thine ire!" indignant Cameron said,
  "Nor let the breezes blow my words away;
"A dire contagion will thy race o'erspread,
  "Thyself, wives, children, all may be its prey;
  "Think of their corses hastening to decay,
"With foul and loathsome blotches on their skin;
  "Nor can the 'Med'cin-man'[a] its progress stay.
"Were thy tribe thick as rain-drops, it would thin
"Thy people and bereave thee of thy dearest kin."

### XXXIV.

"Proud man of Nature! to the 'land of souls,'
  "When the GOOD SPIRIT bids us, we must go;
"That Power by human agency controls
  "Our destinies, whether we've will or no;
  "This truth the elders of thy tribe can show.
"Hither from far beyond the 'Great Salt Lake,'
  "I've come to lessen thy approaching woe;
"But ere this mission I can undertake,
"To STAR-FLOWER's hand and heart thou must all
      claim forsake."

### XXXV.

"Further, White Trader, I shall not dissent;
  "Should the infection quickly on us seize,
"And give its wrathful indignation vent,
  "No power have I its ravage to appease.
"E'en now my blood seems in my veins to freeze,
  "Such dreadful terror doth thy speech inspire;
"But white men read in Mystery-books with ease,
  "And we their knowledge in most things admire;
  "So I my doubts will yield, nor further will enquire.

---

[a] This personage performs the part of priest, physician, and fortune-teller, but chiefly pretends to pass for a sorcerer.

### XXXVI.

'' But can, indeed, thy prophecy be true,
  " When on this robe my little ones have slept?
'' Or does it follow I their sleep shall rue,
  " Since till this hour their wonted health they've
      kept ?
  " Yet have thy words upon my senses crept :
'' Deeply we should the Pest's return deplore,
  " For bitterly our wives have o'er it wept,
'' While countless dead lay strew'd along our shore :
'' STAR-ELOWER I will resign !—I have to say no more."

### XXXVII.

" Then, Morah ! I entreat thee to destroy
  " The cloak thou wearest ; take as pledge my
      hand ;
" To save thy life I will my skill employ ;
  " For I the art of healing understand,
  " And am a " *Med'cin*" in my own far land.
" Thou sufferest inwardly, thy cheek is pale ;
  " The air with sickly pestilence is fann'd ;
" And soon, perchance, 'twill wider range assail ;
" But aught in human power shall thee and thine
      avail.

### XXXVIII.

" Of all the gifts of MANITOU to man,
  " A patient, silent spirit is the best ;
" In deeds of worth, and in this life's brief span,
  " We should not under troubles sink deprest,
  " And cast off our existence, ill or blest :
" Then why, Red-Stoic ! brave the LORD OF BREATH,
  " By drawing thus more closely o'er thy breast
" Thy fever-cloak, that mystery-robe of death ?
" Rash—reckless—mute, alas ! to all thy white friend
      saith."

### XXXIX.

Soon was there ample cause for that proud Chief
　　To mourn the vanity of gaudy gear ;
Soon were his tribe involv'd in mortal grief,
　　For the Plague-spot was spreading far and near ;
　　His wives and kindred, seiz'd with sudden fear,
To distant prairies from his wigwam fled ;
　　Death aim'd at all, as with a single spear ;
Morah his little ones no longer fed ;
Wrapp'd in *that* robe, apart, he rank'd amongst the
　　　　dead.

### XL.

Some chiefs stray'd here and there beneath a tree,
　　In anxious groups, with purpose to decide
What means were best to end their misery ;
　　And some, with apathy or sullen pride,
　　Defied the evil, sought the woods and died.
Wigwams were burnt to purify the air,
　　While women rav'd, or wept, or deeply sigh'd,
Or clung to aught they could, or tore their hair ;
But does the White man now alleviate their despair ?

### XLI.

Yes ; Cameron ceas'd not to afford his aid
　　Amongst the sick, the dying, and the dead ;
But most were more incited to upbraid,
　　Than to observe his counsel ; and thus spread
　　The dire distemper to so great a head.
Ah ! had the Red Men taken timely heed,
　　And by the Christian's sage advice been led,
His skill had haply taught them to succeed
　　The fatal pest to check—the ravage to impede.

### XLII.

They now report some trader cherish'd hate
  Against their tribe, and gave the poison'd cloak
To work their woe; or else it was their fate
  The wrath of AREOUSKI to provoke,
  Whose heavy vengeance thus upon them broke;
The curse had extirpated half their race,
  Before diminish'd, and beneath the yoke
Of strangers, who usurp'd a wrongful place,
Enthrall'd their ancient chiefs and brought them to
    disgrace.

### XLIII.

Why longer tarry in that scene of death,
  Propitious not to love's soft genial flame,
Where in each gale still lurk'd the baleful breath,
  And terror still vibrated through the frame.
  For Cameron had now no further aim,
But to remove to some far distant strand,
  With her, the idol of his soul, whose name
Of STAR-FLOWER was exchang'd with heart and hand,
Before a Christian shrine and in a Christian land.


The sagacious reader may find the groundwork of this poem in
a little prose North-American Indian tale, which appeared some
years ago in one of the interesting numbers of Chambers' Journal.


END OF THE DEATH ROBE.

# ONEEKAH.

———

BENEATH a cloven mountain, where a pine
Threw its tall shadow, in the day's decline,
While yet the golden sunset shed a glow
Of amber light upon the lake below,
In whose clear mirror lilies bent to glance
At their own beauty; 'mid the fair expanse,
Two Indians lay; a small canoe, at rest,
Scarce rais'd a ripple on that calm lake's breast;
O'er them the mountain rear'd its peak on high,
As though it soar'd to meet the gorgeous sky.
One chief, who here had venerable grown,
Had long his habitation fix'd alone;
'Twas rudely thatch'd with reeds, the forest-vine
Would round the porch its tendrils fondly twine.
A jutting crag and small o'erhanging wood,
Guarded the dell in which the wigwam stood;
The clustering foliage, from the north wind screen'd
The wild abode, and shrubberies interven'd.

Some smouldering embers on the grass lay strew'd,
That late had serv'd to dress their simple food;
A scoop'd and unslung gourd, just thrown aside,
Their evening draught had temperately supplied.
More distant lay a hatchet, spear, and bow,
Sign that the warriors fear'd no sudden foe;
A belted deer-skin form'd the veteran's vest,
Leaving his right arm free and bare his breast;
While rich in vivid dyes, with studied care,
The symbol of his tribe was tattoo'd [a] there.
Tall was his figure, left by age unbow'd;
By nature stern, ascetic, simple, proud.
Full ninety snows the hoary chief had told,
One third that time scarce o'er his friend had roll'd;
Reverent as son to sire he too appear'd,
Shewing he lov'd as much as he rever'd.
His dress partook of some superior art,
And foreign fashion bore the chiefest part.
Calmly the time-worn pilgrim of the wood
Address'd the partner of his solitude,
Seeming to task his failing memory:
His words the younger penn'd upon his knee—
An oral record, meant but to embrace
The old traditions of his wandering race,
The which, while telling, he would often pause
With vacant look, no matter what the cause;

---

[a] "Ces couleurs ayant pénétré entre cuir et chair ne s'effacent jamais."—*Relation de la Louisianne*, 1720, p. 13.

Some tender thought might in his mind prevail,
And hence the interruptions in his tale :
While from its lonely roost a timid bird,
Startled, might fluttering through the boughs be heard,
To whose retreat the white-hair'd chief, perchance,
Or both, would cast a half-abstracted glance.
'Twas thus he spake : " I'm like a bow unstrung,
" And worn with use, yet is my memory young!
" My eyes are dim, but inward beams a light
" That shows the past before my present sight.
" Mark me, young friend! I do remember well
" A youth like thee, who by the Huron fell ;
" Yes, he resembled thee, or thou dost *him*,
" Like thee in face, as lusty too in limb.
" 'Tis many years since first the tale was told,
" How powerful he was, how brave, how bold ;
" How dauntlessly the Huron he defied,
" How many foes he slew, how nobly died.
" When he was in his tender infancy,
" His mother slung his cradle to the tree,
" To which, from time to time, she anxious crept,
" To be assur'd her darling safely slept,
" And that the melody of birds had not
" Disturb'd her charge in his suspended cot.
" He grew from childhood by his father's side,
" And well might kindle all a father's pride.
" Soon taught to wield the axe, to poise the spear,
" To dare the warrior, and to chase the deer ;

" Surprise the beaver in the forest dark,
" And to construct the light canoe of bark;
" To track the elk towards the dreary swamp,
" What time the fire-fly trims his tiny lamp;
" To bear the heat and cold, to thirst, and fast,
" To scorn the thought of peril, till 'twas past!
" That boy was mine! still fondly lov'd his name,
" And still remember'd all his early fame;
" But battles thinn'd my tribe! alas, the day!
" My son forsook me, distant foes to slay;
" Then soon adversity his steps pursu'd,
" They trac'd him to his covert in the wood.
" Turning a brooklet's silvery course aside,
" The sand reveal'd, beneath its limpid tide,
" The print of moccasins, too well impress'd;
" The marks were his.   Now, listen, chief, the rest:
" Waylaid upon a bold and bushy steep,
" That overhung a torrent dark and deep,
" A foe he met—with long and doubtful strife
" They clos'd—each sought to take the other's life;
" Unflinchingly they parried blow for blow,
" Neither the victor, neither levell'd low;
" Grasping each scalping lock[a] with furious hold,
" Adown the frightful precipice they roll'd.

---

a Alluded to at page 3, line 4. It is the long lock of hair on the top of the head. The skin on which it grows, being about the size of a crown-piece, constitutes the true scalp. They ornament this solitary lock with beads, silver trinkets, &c. and, on grand occasions, with feathers. See *Weld's Travels.*

" Their fall was broken by a pending tree

" Deep rooted in th' abyss !—my son was free !

" While whirl'd the flood, the foe, convuls'd and weak,

" Was seen no more, though heard his dying shriek.

" The Hurons miss'd their chieftain's form erect,

" But knew not what to think, or what suspect;

" Till lengthen'd absence spread the wide alarm,

" That he had perish'd by some stronger arm.

" My son they'd oft in fierce encounter met,

" And on his head a bounty large was set;

" For, shrewdly did they guess, by him alone

" Their stoutest leader had been overthrown.

" Vengeance they swore, and sought at once to trace

" The victor-hero in his hiding place.

" Ah ! too successful ! on a grassy bed,

" Form'd in a deep recess, his feverish head

" Repos'd—perhaps he dreamt—his toils at end,

" He saw once more his home, wife, child, and friend.

" He woke ! but say, what apparition knelt

" Before him now and on his features dwelt?

" 'Twas she, indeed, his own beloved wife,

" The fond, devoted partner of his life.

" Her faithful steps had follow'd him afar,

" Through forests thick, and 'midst the rage of war;

" And, with a mother's strength, had borne her child,

" Sooth'd in her grief, if but her infant smil'd.

" Avails it not by what strange chance she found

" Her husband stretch'd and sleeping on the ground;

' Suffice it, there her fondest hopes were crown'd.

" Brief was the bliss of that ill-fated hour ;
·'His foes around his secret shelter pour.
" Hear you that shout ? it is their death-halloo!
" They come, they come! save him, Great Manitou!
" That shriek!—it is his wife's—she falls! she dies!
" Whilst o'er their captive shouts exulting rise.
" But let me pause—He burns! Methinks I see
" My boy in that last dire extremity!
" They seiz'd, they bound him, lit the fatal brand,
" The death-pyre blaz'd, as quick they gave command.
" Delighted, too, each quivering wound to sear,
" They ask'd him, taunting, if he felt no fear.
" Amidst his tortures, to the Huron throng
" He thus uprais'd his last and dying song.

## DEATH-SONG.

### I.

" ' The sons of your tribe are all timid and tame,
For children might mock them, and women would
     shame.
*Our* warriors have hearts that still steadfastly brave
The brunt of our foes, as the rocks breast the wave ;
They quail not with fear at the tomahawk's stroke,
They are firm in the storm as the proud forest-oak.
Then feed high the blaze, 'twill your triumph proclaim,
But never your torments shall tarnish my name.
Like cowards ye shrink at an arrow or spear,
And fly at our war-whoop, like timorous deer ;

Though ye vaunt of your courage, ye wait not to try
The strength of your bows when our warriors are nigh.
The sons of your tribe are all timid and tame,
For children might mock them and women would
    shame !


## II.

Had I now at my call but a score of my race,
Ye would flee from their presence and sink in disgrace ;
They would scatter your tribe, as the leaves of the
    trees
In the wind of the " corn-moon " are blown by the
    breeze.
But they know not my fate, or the shafts from their
    bows
Would speedily lessen the ranks of my foes !
Yet they still shall avenge me, and many a fire
Shall blaze for the one in which now I expire !
If a groan ye would hope to extort, 'tis in vain,
For Oneekah was never yet vanquish'd by pain ;
The sires of my line shall not blush for their son,
My life shall be clos'd as it dauntless begun.
The sons of your tribe are all timid and tame,
For children might mock them and women would
    shame ! '


  " Too well did they their usual rites pursue,
" Ingenious still to find some torture new.—

" My friend ! *our* warriors ne'er by signs reveal
" The pangs their bodies may be doom'd to feel.
" He call'd them *squaws*, too weak to hunt their game,
" And bade them mark *his* firm and manly frame.
" At this their furious rage no limits knew,
" A fatal arrow mercifully flew
" And pierc'd the breast their fires could not subdue.—
" 'Tis said his spirit, in its midnight round,
" Points where his bones lie bleaching on the ground ;
" That o'er the lake the breeze still bears along
" His last loud war-whoop, and his dying-song.
" But oft upon that lake my lonely bark
" I've slowly steer'd, when all was still and dark ;
" Or, when the moon sent forth its paly beam,
" I've gently glided down some neighb'ring stream ;
" But ne'er to me did aught disturb the gloom,
" Of sight or sound, except the bittern's boom.
" And thus, young friend, of him, my son, bereft,
" No single remnant of my tribe was left,
" Save he who now recites this mournful tale,
" A lone branch, wither'd, blown by every gale !"

   " Nay, not alone, nor last of all thy race ;
" Look on these features ! canst thou in them trace
" No mark'd resemblance, lineaments, still true
" To those from whom they sprung, my sire ! to you ?"

   " Chief of a stranger-land, oh, mock me not !
" He can no more return to this sad spot !"

" I *mock* thee not, as proof shall well attest,
" My grandsire ! I could weep upon thy breast !
" Listen ! my tongue shall now thine ear arrest :
" While my brave father linger'd on the pyre,
" A white man snatch'd me from the Huron's ire,
" Or I had soon been cast into the fire.
" He bore me to the white man's tents, and there
" Made me the object of his kindest care.
" I learn'd to love him, and, in course of time,
" Lov'd too the speech and customs of his clime.
" But he had also griefs, his health they tried,
" My second father slowly pin'd and died.
" Releas'd from ties, I panted to retrace
" My native wilds, and seek my kindred race ;
" Since then I've sojourn'd with the Huron tribe,
" And oft they still my honor'd sire describe.
" But now that years a softer mood have wrought,
" They only tell how fearlessly he fought,
" And how, when hemm'd by fate on every side,
' Like a true Indian, undismay'd he died.
" A friendly chieftain, at my keen desire,
" Sent of my father's nation to enquire ;
" From him some scanty information came,
" He learn'd one aged man still bore my name.
" Through tangled forests and through bushy brake,
" Where lurks, in glittering coils, the secret snake,
" Ready to seize the unresisting prey
" That comes within the circle of his sway,—

" I've toil'd, till here I found thy leafy bow'r ;
" Henceforth, my care to soothe thy latest hour."
He paus'd, then knelt upon the grassy mound,
The old man bent *his* knee ; his look profound
Told more than could his mute-struck tongue impart,
The voiceless language of a bursting heart ;
Tears down his furrow'd cheeks began to flow,
But not of joy alone, nor yet of woe ;
For he was Spirit-humbled—ne'er before
Did he the God of Christians thus adore.
But now an instantaneous light, refin'd,
Remov'd the film from his benighted mind.
The hoary chief, so long by sorrow bent,
Felt as if some kind angel had been sent
Above his grave, to chant a last lament.
" Heaven will'd thy mission to my dwelling-place,"
He said, " and saves a scion of my race !"
As thus he spake, the youth he linger'd o'er,
Murmur'd a blessing, and then breath'd no more.

THE END.

K

# A SCENE

## BANKS OF LAKE HURON.

———

"They are now forgot in their land; their tombs are not found on the heath. Years came on with their storms. The green mounds are mouldered away."—Vide *Poems of Ossian.*

———

WHERE the tall thick o'erhanging forest threw,
In shadows wide, its green but sombre hue,
Two chiefs, of giant form and high degree,
Reflecting, sat beneath an aged tree ;
The scene was still, the air was soft and sweet,
And sleeping lay Lake Huron at their feet.
Strange was the garb the hunter-warrior wore,
But picturesque and meet to that wild shore.
The younger one, of light and vigorous frame,
Whose eye flash'd forth a fierce and darkling flame,
Wore, on his painted breast, a jaguar's hide,
Which, o'er his shoulders, to his girt was tied ;

Red were his leggings, o'er his ankles thin
Was drawn the fring'd and pliant moccasin ;
His manly head of all its locks was bare,
Except a solitary tuft of hair,
Which, brightly streaming, of a jetty black,
And deck'd with feathers, wav'd adown his back,
Where arrows and a hiccory bow were brac'd ;—
A beaded wampum-belt, around his waist
A polish'd hatchet held, and sheathless knife,
Too often wielded to the waste of life.

The other chief, by deepen'd furrows, told
That many winters o'er his head had roll'd ;
Yet still his form appear'd to mock at time,
He look'd the Guardian Genius of his clime ;
Down from his neck a bear-skin wrapp'd him round,—
Mid-high, by bison-thongs grotesquely bound,—
So ample, when he stood, it trail'd the ground.
Calm was his brow, o'er which some grey hairs stream'd,
Thoughtful his look, though still his dark eye gleam'd
With lingering fire, while sedulous to lend
His fix'd attention to his youthful friend,
Who thus, in accents half suppress'd and wild,
The hoary chieftain's pensive thoughts beguil'd.

" A Voice above our hills may yet arrest
" Those White Men who have long our tribes oppress'd.

" Ere them we saw, we roam'd, unscath'd, at will;

" Free were our wood-wilds, free they should be still !

" What have they taught us that we wish'd to know?

" Before they came, we strung th' unerring bow;

" Before they came, we carv'd the birch canoe ;

" Swift were our arrows and sharp-pointed too !—

" Say, was the grass less green ? the storm less felt?

" Is wool more warm than is the wild-bear's pelt ?

" Are our firm bodies, shielded from the cold

" By flimsy rags, more hardy or more bold ?

" Kind Nature gave us boundless space to roam,

" And, wheresoe'er we chose, a charter'd home.

" What are we now ? despis'd our ev'ry claim,

" A scatter'd race, without a home or name !

" With peaceful words, but treachery accurst,

" They came—alas ! we knew them not at first !

" In huge pirogues they left their distant shores,

" To tempt us with their glittering, worthless stores,

" Baubles that seem'd to our untutor'd sight

" Like gems from Nature's mines, as rare as bright :

" With these and worse, their fire-drink, deadly, dire,

" They conquer'd, more than with their tubes of fire.

" Too soon, too easily, we yielded all,

" Obedient, passive, to their tyrant thrall.

" A time there was when all our tribes, content,

" Knew not the common scourge we now lament :

" Our quarrels were our own ; we fought not then

" For rule, or avarice, like these white men.

" An ample plot of ground our wants supplied,
" Nor fish the streams, nor furs the woods denied ;
" Our hardy pleasures gave us strength and health,
" And these to us were still our best of wealth.
" We knew not then that indolence and ease
" Will weaken manhood—more than e'en disease ;
" Then beauteous was each Huron-Maiden's cheek,
" Her sparkling eyes, her tresses glossy, sleek ! "
He paus'd—perhaps the thought of some lov'd maid
At that sad moment o'er his memory stray'd.
The elder chieftain for a moment eyed
The youth, and then in pensive tones replied :

" My son, thou speakest right ! long toils and pains
" We've borne, but to increase the ' pale one's ' gains !
" The rivers yielded fish, the forest deer,
" Our prey was slain where'er we hurl'd the spear ;
" Though dark our glance, and darker, too, our skin,
" The white-fac'd men have blacker hearts within !
" Thou speakest true—through prairies once our own
" We wander now like strangers, scatter'd, lone !
" Through childhood's paths we stray with lingering look,
" And sigh where stood the wigwam by the brook ;
" Or where is seen some moss-grown heap of stones,
" To mark the spot where rest our fathers' bones ;
" Or where the vision of the dance, the chase,
" The warrior's deeds, the maiden's softer grace,
" Recall the days that still in memory dwell,
" And sadly make this aged bosom swell !

" Where, where is she, my own, my faithful wife,
" Ah! once the joy and solace of my life?
" By White Men's hand the fatal blow was giv'n,
" Through which her spirit from my side was riv'n,
" To dwell, GREAT MANITOU! with thee in heav'n!"

Thus Age and Youth, amidst their native wild,
After the toils of chase, an hour beguil'd.
Within their woodland haunt, beneath the pine,
They watch'd the glowing Evening's sun decline;
Meanwhile the soothing pipe its light wreath spread,
Till each, in twilight, sought his matted bed.

FINIS.

J. MALLETT, PRINTER, WARDOUR STREET, SOHO, LONDON.